Annabel Gray

**A Romance of Regent Street**

A Novel: Vol. I.

Annabel Gray

**A Romance of Regent Street**
*A Novel: Vol. I.*

ISBN/EAN: 9783337067779

Printed in Europe, USA, Canada, Australia, Japan

Cover: Foto ©Andreas Hilbeck / pixelio.de

More available books at **www.hansebooks.com**

# A ROMANCE OF REGENT STREET.

## A NOVEL.

By ANNABEL GRAY,

AUTHOR OF 'MARGARET DUNBAR,' 'WAIT AND WIN,' 'AMARANTH' MYSTERY,' ETC.

*IN THREE VOLUMES.*

VOL. I.

TINSLEY BROTHERS,
CATHERINE STREET, STRAND,
LONDON.

———

1881.

TO

MY BROTHER,

𝕵𝖆𝖒𝖊𝖘 𝖂𝖆𝖙𝖓𝖊𝖞 𝖂𝖎𝖑𝖘𝖔𝖓,

THIS WORK IS

AFFECTIONATELY DEDICATED.

# CONTENTS.

## CHAPTER VII.

## CHAPTER VIII.

## CHAPTER IX.

## CHAPTER X.

## CHAPTER XI.

## CHAPTER XII.

## CHAPTER XIII.

## CHAPTER XIV.

## CHAPTER XV.

# A ROMANCE OF REGENT STREET.

## CHAPTER I.

### LOMBY'S CIRCUS.

'There be some with serpent eyes,
Hearted like the snake which lies
Cold beneath warm summer skies.'

RAIN everywhere. Nothing but rain. It had fallen for days and weeks in dreary, drizzling showers, so that people talked of fine weather and sunshine as if they belonged to another planet, and had naught in common with this earth of ours.

The inhabitants of the little village of Brooksmere, a secluded spot in the pastoral county of Devonshire, shook their heads, thinking of the troubles and losses of the agriculturalists, the prospect of a bad harvest, the ruin of the hay crops, the blight of the hops, the bad state of trade, and the miserable season.

When would this unfortunate rain cease? It descended in sluggish unconcern for the welfare of those whose fortunes it was destroying. It soaked the lanes and fields, and from drenching the hawthorns in May, it spoilt the corn in September.

Some wiseacres in the Brooksmere village declared that two planets were nearer the sun than usual; others foretold a great wave of heat that would speedily reduce us all to the pleasant condition of cinders.

Bishops and priests had prayers offered up in their churches and chapels for fine weather, with very little result save a few fierce Promethean storms.

It was now falling, this pitiless rain, on the sixteen golden cars and limp, if glorious, flags comprising a portion of Lomby's magnificent and world-renowned Imperial Circus, that was about to entertain the villagers of Brooksmere with a performance to last 'three days only.'

It was dropping on the sixteen golden cars in which the animals were being conveyed to their destination in a wet corner of the common called 'Mad Acre End.' It angered the elephants, giving violent influenza to the 'Baby,' a mild young party called Alonzo, shaping later on to be a very promising specimen of elephantine artistic training. Even the tigers looked on more sulkily than usual at their damp bars, and a very magnificent lion, 'Marengo,' one of the leading attractions of 'Lomby's Imperial Circus,' had been heard to cough in a more distressingly consumptive manner than altogether favoured the hope of his obtaining longevity.

The dead leaves were strewing the road in little fluttering heaps as the sixteen cars passed onwards. The band tried to be lively, and with the aid of a cornet, gave several weird and unearthly variations on an air resembling 'Grandfather's Clock,' for the sixteen cars, with their long-tailed horses and well-trained ponies, and numerous *employés*, were bound to pass on their way, if not exactly rejoicing, at least with outward philosophical precision and serenity.

Among the women who formed more or less star artistes and astronomical luminaries of the great circus was one pre-eminent above all in daring, if not in grace. She had beauty of the full-blooded kind, however, that gives redness to the cheeks and thickness to the skull ; the same, we may see, that the great

Flemish painter delighted in—a gross, bone-less, unintellectual order of loveliness.

A curious woman, this Madame Juanita, tall of stature, with a somewhat broad waist, that had of late proved fatal to the grace of her equestrian performances, features well-cut and regular, a cold, crafty smile, a harsh and cruel mouth. She was Spanish, and had the low, retreating forehead of the south, suggesting heavy ignorance and dulness; there might be fire in her large dark eyes, but it was not lit from the soul. The fire was kindled by spite or passion, or ignoble triumph. Her hair was jet black, waxed and gummed to perfection—she always wore it neatly plaited and plastered down, and if it were not quite so clean as it might have been, it shone as nicely as well-polished ebony.

A sensualist might have pronounced her charming—a fine woman. ' Ah, *belle femme !* ' for, as regards the senses, we invariably like those who resemble ourselves, and a wife is, or ought to be, the counterpart of her spouse.

This was Juanita Dalton, the circus master's wife, and the protectress of Nellie Raymond.

The sixteen cars were now encamped on that delightful corner of the common called ' Mad Acre End,' and Madame Juanita was helping herself to huge slices of a well-baked grouse pie, to which she seemed to be doing ample justice.

The tents were pitched, the rain defied, the lions were roaring, the clown was feeding his motherless baby in one of the stalls set apart for the Chesterfield colt—a superb stallion that Jack Dalton advertised had been presented to him by the Emperor of China—when Nellie passed along by the Arabian horse's hoofs and approached Ludovico—the assumed name of the clown—a reckless, good-hearted fellow. His real cognomen was Ben Lorton.

Nellie's form, height, and complexion were of the purest English type. Picture a clear, oval face, a broad and candid forehead, shaded in with an abundance of brown curls, touched here and there with burnished gold, falling about a pair of shoulders and small, exquisitely modelled bust. There was nothing solid, prim, or majestic in her girlish figure ; it seemed rather to have been cramped and starved in extreme childhood, so that maturity must arrive late, or as if the childish eyes had waited so long for happiness to come into them that the often repressed tears had gathered into a cloud, and gave that mournful look to the iris.

Touches of rare sweetness and feeling came and went about the lips, and softened the lines of the mouth that was so chiselled by nature's master-hand, it seemed made for kisses. Full, rather pouting lips that took away the peculiar spirituality of the brow, gave Nellie the appearance of possessing more materialism and liveliness than the thoughtful, wearied expression indicated at a first glance.

'You seem very fond of the baby,' Nellie said, as she watched Ludovico dip a leaden spoon in some sopped bread and milk.

The clown was always puzzled by Nellie's ways and looks and manner of speech. She never swore or drank, or made love to any one. There was no leer in her large dark blue eyes, with their modest luminance.

'Why shouldn't I be fond of him, bless his little 'eart?' the clown remarked, his left eye straying towards the open tent where Madame Juanita was licking both the inside of the platter and her own dusky fingers alternately.

Nellie sat down on a rough and hastily manufactured manger apportioned to the Chesterfield colt, that gentlemanly but eccentric stallion not having yet put in an appearance, and having been a little awkward and aggressive on the road, had broken a stationer's large plate-glass window, and kicked a well-meaning crossing-sweeper and his broom into a drain.

' I never remember any one being kind to me, Ludovico,' Nellie said after a pause ; ' not even when I was quite a little girl. I do so often wonder who I am, and where my father and mother are.'

' Oh, my dear, wot can that matter now ? It's wot we do at the present which signifies. I dessays you came out of a union,' said Ludovico, lifting his thin, bloodless hand, and shaking the baby to make it the better swallow a piece of soaked crust, ' or mebbe one of yer parents was 'ung.'

' I can only remember Madame Juanita all these long years. She gave me my first lessons on the tight-rope, and the marks of the rope she thrashed me with, because I fell twice, made me learn to count my numbers up to ten. That was how I first learnt figures. There were two other acrobats besides me. One died. I wished, oh, how I wished, it had been me.'

' Poor child,' said the clown, ' wishing ain't no good. For instance, you might be afraid o' performin' with Herebus and Don Pedro in public. I sees ye among 'em plucky enough when we are by ourselves, but ye'd 'ave to do it, Nellie, straight away, if you was ordered. Ye'd wish and wish Madame

Juanita might die, and never beat you any more, and never want ye to show yourself to a big haudience with Herebus and Don Pedro, but wishing won't—'

Nellie sprang from the manger, every trace of listlessness and indifference in her manner at an end.

'Ludovico, don't say it—don't say she means to make me perform with the tigers, because my breath comes and goes so quickly, and my heart beats, and their eyes will seem to have a different meaning then, and oh, Ludovico, I am afraid—'

'Why, Nell, my gal, afraid? That's a pretty word for our best and boldest rider. The Chesterfield colt ain't here, and so—'

'It isn't the horses nor the ponies that I mind, and I'd trust the lions—they're blind and old and tame, but there's something in the others, in their very movements and their walk, even when they crouch, so fierce and untameable that I dread, and they know it. They're waiting for me—they will kill me.'

'She's but a girl,' said Ludovico. 'It's natural, and they're ugly beasts. I'm clean again' such tricks and performances, Nellie.

'I remember seeing two pictures long ago in a shop window in Regent Street, which gave me this bad turn, and set me against the business,' said Nellie, her voice trembling. 'One was the picture of a place, something like our circus, except that fine ladies and gentlemen were all in boxes around, and somebody had dropped a rose near the lions, and a girl in white went in to pick it up; but that picture didn't upset me like the other, for I'd have done the same.'

Nellie now waved her arm in the air to give better effect to her words.

'This other picture was like a circus, too; but it made my blood curdle in my veins to look at it. There were lions and tigers, just like ours, but they were fierce and savage beasts from the deserts, and they were mangling human forms; bones lay about, arms and hands wrenched and torn. A beautiful girl, with her hands tied, afforded a meal to one; an old man, with white hair, for another, and I shrieked out all of a sudden, Ludovico—I don't know why—I'd never seen a picture of our animals before, and I never quite knew their nature, but a horror of the circus seized me. A young gentleman who was passing watched me. He was very kind, for when I fainted he took me safely home in a cab. I was always seeing that beautiful young girl, and the blood on the tiger's tusks, even in my dreams. It gave me an illness. No, I will never perform in public with Erebus and Don Pedro. Never at the bidding of a woman I hate—'

' Nellie Raymond, come here !'

It was Madame Juanita's voice.

' Is this a nursery?' she said, with a dry, bitter curl of the lip, addressing the clown. ' Is there nothing better for you to do than dawdle and feed a brat, and idle your time away with Nellie ? And now, miss, a word with you.'

She carried a small riding-whip in her hand, which she brought down several times in succession on Nellie's white shoulders.

' Thus much for your idleness.  So you hate me, do you ?'

Long repressed rebellion and pain forced angry words from Nellie's lips.

She wheeled round on her tyrant, and clasped her slender hands.

' I do hate you !  A crueller mistress, a more barbarous woman—a greater fiend in human shape cannot exist.'

' Hush, Nellie, hush,' another voice here cried, coming behind them.  ' It's only bilious spite, child.'

This was Lepelletier, a ' character,' a mesmerist, a man of science, deemed half mad or crazed by the *troupe*, the fortunes of which he had never shared, having merely travelled with them for a caprice.

'You hear her?' cried madame, addressing Lepelletier.

The scene had still a curious eastern tone. Madame Juanita was of herself a picture, with the sullen rage on her heavy brows.

'I will not stay with you,' said Nellie more quietly. 'Why not leave the very hardest lot fate could deal one?'

'Excellent,' said the mesmerist. 'That is logic. The girl has reason; dearest Juanita, be patient.'

He laid his hand on her shoulder.

Nellie, now looking up, saw a man, hardly taller than herself, his features suffused with fury. This was a Cuban, Ferrara by name, part manager of the circus; Dalton's bosom friend, money-lender, and ally.

Lepelletier, stepping back, also saw this savage face, dark and swarthy with passion. Madame Juanita, true coquette and type of her race, gloried in the Cuban's fury. It was purely physical, and to her taste.

'Why do you touch her shoulder?' the Cuban hissed.

'Ah, Ferrara, is it you?' said the mesmerist, lightly.

He subjugated the tyrant Juanita mentally, the other by sheer brute force.

'Yes, it is I, and some day you will answer for this with your life.'

Madame Juanita smiled.

'*Mon ange,*' said Lepelletier, disregarding the Cuban's words, believe me, you look handsomer in your rage ; in correcting this rebellious girl just now, that narrow, yet ivory brow seemed to expand with hate and wrath. You were superb, brutal, destructive, but when you smile you may look elated and content, but commonplace—believe me, commonplace. You perceive how I cherish your glances, actions, and tones.'

'*Tu est bête,*' cried Madame Juanita, who was just then more in the mood to appreciate the attentions of Ferrara ; she turned and left the stable with him.

Lepelletier now glanced at Nellie. She had understood the subtle contempt in his voice.

The mesmerist scrutinised the girl more closely.

'I suppose you believe that the time has come for you to strike for liberty,' he said, addressing her suddenly.

'Yes,' said Nellie stolidly, 'I mean to go.'

'And if caught and again caged, remember you are hers by the law as much as she is Dalton's by marriage. You were apprenticed to her, you are her slave,—nearly as much so as any African bought of old in the market. She has fed and clothed you for

years, given you her protection,—I see by
the curl of that pretty lip it has not pleased
you,—had you instructed in a profession
which, if not one of the noblest and most
elevating, will provide you with means of
living, and yet you are ungrateful.'

'I will leave her,' said Nellie, half distracted with doubts and fears. 'I will go to
a magistrate, show him some of her blows,
tell him of her vices, her lawless—'

'Bah! An employer may chastise her
apprentice when she sees fit, and a magistrate is not a Lycurgus or a Solon. You
have no case. You are not particularly
starved-looking, or pale, or withered. This
arm is plump, so also is the neck and throat.
Stay and endure your lot.'

Lepelletier seemed amused with the quivering lights and shades passing so quickly in
succession over Nellie's features.

'So you don't admire Madame Juanita?
That superb, that majestic form, imperial as
a Juno or Lucretia, inspires you with no
admiration ; the neatly-dressed ebon hair
(yours is, I see, very straggling and untidy ;
but you English girls, if clean, are so careless), glossy as one of the tiger's coats, never
makes you envious of her superior trimness,
—never makes you see the superiority of
her charms over yours, you poor, tender,

romantic, unformed child! Think of those chiselled features,—the flashing teeth, the red cheeks, the coquettish dimples, and then say, Nellie, whether I, as a sometime favoured admirer, do not run a serious risk of meeting my death at the hands of the amorous Cuban ? '

' Monsieur Lepelletier, why do you stay with us ? ' said Nellie. ' Your life must be detestable.'

' *Du tout,*' he answered. ' See, then, I am forty-five, and am the heir to a marquisate. I have lived, like all Frenchmen, with beautiful disregard of fine codes, and then I fall in love. I am mad, wretched, impassioned ; I am a gambler and mesmerist, and come to a circus instead of a madhouse, because there is change, freedom, excitement, and beauty. Think of madame! My dear child, she is calling for you at this very moment.'

He turned to draw a cigarette from his pocket, lighted it, and nodding farewell to Nellie, sauntered towards a caravan of panthers.

' He will not stretch out a helping hand,' murmured the girl ; ' he is as heartless as the rest.'

# CHAPTER II.

### ALONE IN THE WORLD.

'She whose nude shoulders and long golden hair,
  Slow cradled by the undulating tide,
  Shone in the early sunlight of the dawn.'

MADAME JUANITA was not alone when Nellie obeyed her summons and entered the tent. The Cuban sat writing at a little table, and madame was engaged in melting down some fresh gum and wax for her hair, the rain having soaked through a light wicker basket in which she carried the various aids and appliances set apart for her peculiar beauty, and spoilt the contents of a neat-looking little pot, over the destruction of which she heaved some deep and tragic sighs.

Nellie looked very youthful and fair in her timid hesitation and rich, varying colour, as she entered the tent. The weals on her white neck were still there, bright red lines swollen above the surface of the skin; but there was something new in her expression to be read even by such a mere animal as Madame Juanita. Dulness and ignorance have often keen instincts. Madame swore a few brutal oaths to herself in Spanish as she summoned Nellie to her side.

'You called me?' said Nellie, indifferently.

'Insolent!' muttered the Spaniard, fanning herself. 'Do you forget who you are speaking to?'

The girl had no physical fear of any thing created. Her dread lay deeper than this; for she had learnt to shrink from the malice of that severe and vindictive eye, the perfidious leer, the unintelligence of the low, narrow forehead. How could she contend against the low forces of the small, cramped mind—the invisible agency of characteristics beyond her ken?

Madame Juanita had turned her short neck round very rapidly as she addressed Nellie, and the hectoring tone she invariably adopted increased in fury. The Cuban lifted his head and glared at Nellie with marked displeasure.

M. Lepelletier, still smoking his cigarette outside, lounged towards the tent, smiling, and unperceived by those inside, listened to every word.

'It isn't likely I should forget that,' said
Nellie, her lip quivering.

She was naturally nervous and excitable. The flame of her rage and impulse
was dying out, leaving her cold again.

'Are you aware that you will perform in
public to - night with Erebus and Don
Pedro?' asked the Spaniard, in measured
tones.

Nellie turned deadly pale, and griped
the edge of the table. A sullen glance of
triumph in this mute agony was read by
Nellie, and rekindled the flame. Walking
towards to her torturer, she said, clearly and
distinctly,—

'I wish to leave the circus to-night, and
I will.'

She set her teeth hard. Madame's triumphant glance died out in malice.

'You will, will you? Pretty words!—
nice temper!'

Nellie shrank back a little, partly from
habit; but her mettlesome heart soon con-
quered the timidity engendered by long ill-
usage. She went on now quite calmly,—

'This is England. It is a free land; and
I lead a dog's life. Soon it will kill me. I
do not wish to die, for I am young. I have
worked years for you without wages, often
without food. Now you seek to murder me,

and I will not stay ; you may find another apprentice.'

The changes in madame's face grew still darker and more tragic as Nellie spoke. That free, wild spirit of the wretched girl addressed her in a new fashion. If it was English it was very strange ; it must be crushed.

'I only wish you were an animal,' gasped Madame Juanita. 'How I'd pay you out then ! Santa Madonna !'

She took down a powerful horsewhip hanging above her head, and cracked it two or three times in an ominous manner in the air, and still the colour rose brighter in Nellie's cheeks, and a furious fire burnt in her ever mournful eyes.

'Only let her touch me,' thought Nellie ; 'she shall find her match at last.'

'You will not take Erebus and Don Pedro into the circus ? You decline to obey me— you, my apprentice, bought with good gold when you were a whining brat !'

Her fury here nearly choked her, and the lash of the whip just touched Nellie's golden-brown curls.

Without an instant's hesitation the girl rushed up to her, wrenched the weapon from her hand, bent it on the ground, broke it into three separate pieces, and threw them at her. She was sobbing with passion, her look quite wild and overwrought.

Lepelletier now advanced a step. He had been a witness of the whole proceedings.

'Devilish plucky little thing!' he muttered, and lit a fresh cigarette.

The Cuban had thrown down his pen, and running up to Nellie, seized her hands, and tried, but ineffectually, to tie them behind her back.

Strange to say, Madame Juanita was now calm and controlled. She was laughing under her breath—not pleasantly, but with the sort of mirth we might suppose a well-fed boa-constrictor might indulge in when looking at a lamb, and too lazy to descend the tree to kill.

'I think we had better leave her alone,' said Madame Juanita, as Nellie's breast heaved and fell.

Like all tyrants and bullies, she was a coward.

Nellie now advanced again to the Spaniard, the tone of her voice harsher and more metallic.

'I told you that I wished to leave the circus to-night, and I will; but I have changed my mind about the tigers. I will undertake to promise the public a fine entertainment—rare sport—excitement, novelty, sensation!

Oh, great heaven, that it must only end one way!'

She sank down on her knees, her hands clasped, the autumnal light on her features, the rain still dripping on the canvas of the tents with incessant downpour.

'This is carrying pluckiness too far,' muttered Lepelletier. 'I will not allow this girl with her nimbus of golden-brown hair to be mangled like a martyr. I must try and find her a home.'

'Juanita,' now called a voice from a distant tent, 'do you know what time it is? Why, in another hour the performance will begin. Nellie— Why, where's Nell?'

It was Jack Dalton who spoke, patting the arched neck of the Chesterfield colt, which slashed out its hind legs and tried to make its white teeth brand the circus-master's muscular arm.

'Ain't he a pretty villain!' asked Dalton, his hat on one side. 'Oh, beautiful! Look at his points; there ain't a 'orse in any living equestrian *troupe* and variety entertainment in all England as 'll beat him.

The magnificent Juanita, her scowling brows as dark as night, now approached the Chesterfield colt, passing her hand first over his hocks and then fetlocks, like a professional vet.

'I think you better let me ride him,' she said, meaningly. 'I know I carry flesh, but I'm not yet cursed with no more figure than a sponge, and he wants riding, yes, and my fancy bit. I tell you what, Jack,' she continued, winking her eye, which indeed gave it a very diabolical twist—it was of the large, well-opened, indolent kind—'Nellie's one too many for us; she flew at me to-day, and broke a horsewhip into pieces, and threw them into my face.'

'You allays was a deuced sight too 'ard on the girl. Ain't she a-goin' to appear? She draws, there's no denyin' it—just seventeen—and that gold-brown 'air, it's worth anything over white muslin. I 'ope Nell won't cut the pro—'

'Obstinate and insolent little minx!'

Madame Juanita hated this praise; it was gall and wormwood to her vanity.

'But she'll go to Pontet's *troupe* if she leaves us. Pontet'll bid double; he'll keep 'er in clover, I tell ye, and d'ye think Nellie's such a fool as to stay to be whipped by you?'

Madame Juanita found these questions unanswerable. She returned to her tent and prepared her toilet for the evening, and then— some strong, black coffee, swallowing grounds and all in her anger.

Meanwhile, Nellie, on her knees before a little trunk, was looking over some articles —relics and presents, maybe, but all of a simple, humble sort—a sticky valentine, sent years ago by a young lover, a boy rider, who had loved her, and died of a heavy fall.

'Poor Artie!' the girl muttered, 'he was very good to me; he used to talk of the time when we should both be grown-up, and could be married. I remember how he died alone in the garret, holding my hand.'

She kissed the valentine softly, and replaced it in the trunk. Turning round, she saw Jack Dalton, the circus-master. Her neck and arms were bare, for she was in the midst of dressing for her performance with the tigers, but superfine feelings of bashfulness were never encouraged in the circus. Nellie did not blush; why should she? She looked upon the brawny-armed, muscular Jack Dalton as a semi-guardian and protector.

'Got the miserables, 'ave you, little Nell?' he said thoughtfully. 'So you've quarrelled with Juanita. Well, she is a brute, I know it—who better?'

'She is your wife, sir,' Nellie ventured to remark.

'And don't I know that to my cost, too?

What an armful, but a fine woman, eh, Nell?'

'Yes, sir,' Nellie responded indifferently, preparing to curl her hair, prior to donning her muslin frock.

She was thinking of the picture in Regent Street, of the man who had seen her safely home, and left her with a languid smile; a man very different to the set who patronised Lomby's Circus. Nellie had even tried to draw his features from memory on the fly-leaf of a faded copy of Milton's *Comus*, which she had found knocking about one of the tents.

Jack Dalton thought Nellie's one of the fairest faces he had ever gazed on; but he had never sought any disreputable means of perverting her innocence. The circus-master had stood her friend and protector all these years, and although she could remember no life unassociated with the circus, its gross-ness and brutality had never obliterated the natural grace and innocency of her nature.

'So I 'ear you're goin' to leave us, Nellie. I'm sorry for it, but I 'ope you've got a few kind farewell words for me ere parting.'

'I have, indeed, sir,' said Nellie, grate-fully extending her hand.

He thought her strangely pale—what he

termed ‘queer’ in her ways and looks to-
night.

‘ I want to ask you one thing before I go,
sir,’ Nellie went on quickly. ‘ Madame
Juanita never would answer me fair. Tell
me, before we part, something about the
mystery of my lot—something about my
father and mother, and how you came with
your apprentice.’

Dalton burst into a hearty laugh.

‘ There’s romance for ye. Want to ’ear
yer family ’istory ? Fancy, perhaps, ye’re
descended from the Plantagenets, or the
Montmerancis, and that fry. Why, my dear,
you come out of a cellar !’

‘ A cellar ?’ re-echoed Nellie ; then shaking her head, ‘ I don’t believe it.’

‘ Well, leastways, we bought ye out of
one. A young woman was a nursin’ ye, and
an old ’un a lookin’ on. I says, “ We wants a
kid to rear for the pro’,” and the two looks
at one another, and the old ’un ups
and says, “ Take Nellie ; we’re off to
America, and don’t want the brat ; no
one’ll inquire or make a row. What’ll yer
give ?” ’

‘ Wanted, Nellie Raymond,’ here a boy’s
voice called.

‘ I must go,’ said Nellie. ‘ Good-bye, Mr
Dalton !’

She offered him her hand. He was startled at hearing himself also volubly called by his wife, and ran out into the open shed.

'I shall die,' muttered Nellie, lingering a moment, and drawing her hand over her brow, 'and better so. Born in a cellar to die in a circus—'

'Nellie Raymond, are you coming?' again shrieked the boy. 'The audience are stampin' like mad.'

She hesitated no longer, but passing quickly by the Arabs, saw the large cage in which Don Pedro and Erebus were walking restlessly to and fro. The paper garlands and wreaths were near; the red hoops and their glittering stars shone in the gaslight. Nellie made her customary bow to the audience, kissed the tips of her fingers to them amid deafening applause, and looking herself like a picture of Lileth—but, alas! exiled from Paradise—with her golden-brown curls floating below her waist, ascended the steps and entered the cage.

'My, she's a beauty!' a young man remarked, pensively, contemplating Nellie's profile.

'It makes one's blood run cold, though, to see her with the tigers, don't it?'

'Oh, my dear, she's used to it, depend

upon it.   They've all had their teeth pulled out, and been drugged with opium, or stunned with red-hot pokers.'

These were some of the remarks passing round.

At that moment Erebus, shaking himself, slightly yawned.   The great grim teeth flashed before their eyes.   It was Nellie's business to make this sulky brute jump once more through the last hoop.   Don Pedro had resigned himself with all the philosophy of the noble savage to his fate ; he had allowed himself to be crowned with laurel wreaths till he almost resembled some antique Roman conqueror, and he looked at Nellie with quite a benevolent air, as if the whip she flourished over his head were a plaything.

The audience at this point cheered vo-ciferously.   Nellie already felt relieved— all might end well.   Erebus alone eyed her savagely, even defiantly.   She held the hoop and dealt him a rather smart blow with the whip for his unwillingness to leap through it, but at that moment, looking up, Nellie caught sight of the same man she had seen in Regent Street when watching the picture of the blood-stained arena and the martyrs' bodies, and all her old horror and nervous agony seized her.

The whip fell from her hand, Erebus growled, Don Pedro blinked amiably, and shook off four wreaths in succession ; people started to their feet ; some shuddered. Jack Dalton, looking on from the wings, saw something wrong had happened.

'Come and save her !' he roared to several men grouped round, and was just rushing on to the circus when Erebus sprang at Nellie, struck her down, and clawed her shoulder.

The audience screamed, women sobbed— they saw the dark stream of blood flowing over her neck as Jack Dalton bore her in his arms senseless from the cage.

The man who had caused Nellie's emotion, and witnessed the accident, now appeared with a doctor who offered his services.

'Bah ! a mere scratch !' sneered Madame Juanita, in her tight black velvet riding-habit, patting the neck of the Chesterfield colt.

'The wound is not very deep, and she will do well,' the doctor said, taking out a case of instruments, and requesting some warm water and a sponge to be quickly brought.

Nellie shivered, opened her lips, and then her eyes—to meet a grave, thoughtful glance ; but the shock had been too severe. She fainted again.

The man glided away, and was soon lost

amidst the crowd.  He had not recognised in Nellie Raymond the same young girl who had been seized with an hysterical attack in Regent Street, and to seek for romance among those attached to a circus was about the last thing he desired.

After Nellie had been conveyed to her little rough bed in one of the distant tents, the wound carefully dressed, and some stimulants applied that thoroughly restored her senses, she glanced round with that determined air which announces a purpose to be carried out.

Nellie was not subject to fainting.  This was, indeed, the second time only in her life that collapse had taken place ; but she was nervous by temperament, quick-witted, and excitable, Great mental distress had undermined her nervous system, but physical fear she knew not.

And now, raising herself on her hard flock pillow, what does she resolve ?

To escape — to cover her bespangled muslin frock with that heavy cloak hanging across some ropes and hoops, and flee into the darkness and rain.  She had a horror of being again cowed into submission by Madame Juanita.

'Now is my only chance,' muttered Nellie, her face pale with the pain of her torn shoulder. 'I will escape, and trust to chance to save me from destruction.'

It still rained, and ' Mad Acre End' looked the very reverse of a tempting spot in which to plunge through the driving rain and impenetrable darkness ; but Nellie, covered with the heavy cloak, rushed into the night, pausing once to look back at the circus, the subdued lights of which through the canvas making it resemble some pale moon amid ebon surroundings.

Her hair, drenched and soaked with the rain, lay matted about her throat, fever in her veins, rebellion in her heart. She was in the mood of that fair Gostanza who had taken a boat and drifted over the waveless seas, praying death might come ; only Nellie wanted to reach the village. She had a few shillings in the little leather purse she had placed in the bosom of her dress, and to secure some humble night's lodging was her present intent. But Nellie did not understand the route. The windings of the heath and common puzzled her ; her feet ached from contact with the harsh stubble and swampy parts, till she feared she might sink and be engulfed.

Presently a dim haze appeared ; it was a river, and here the girl's strength failed her, for by this river she paused, staggered, and fell.

# CHAPTER III.

MR FACULTY FOGG ADDRESSES THE OUTCAST.

'What is this feeling makes me so glad?
Pain that delights me? How can it be—
Pleasure that pains me, fettered though free?'

WHEN Nellie awoke from her swoon, she saw that she had left the reedy swamps of the common far behind. The azure gleams of morning were just touching the wavelets of the river, clouds of pale, diaphanous hues were drifting lazily above her head, and soft winds came and went dreamily, fitful as Diana's breath and kisses when she woke Endymion from his slumber—heralds also of liberty and freedom.

Yes, here at last was liberty—escape from a hateful doom, coarse voices, vulgar scenes, degrading vices.

To wander to the village, to expend her few shillings in buying food and shelter, and then to seek a situation—this was the only plan presenting itself to her mind.

Jack Dalton's words regarding her birth and parentage had, in truth, robbed the girl of any hope she may have cherished as to his affording her some clue to the lives of those people to whom she owed nothing but her bare existence.

Abandoned by father and mother, and sold to a circus proprietor, she could find no intricate web in which to seek her relatives, and whether the daughter of a duchess or a beggar, she at least knew that, like other slaves, she must submit to the exigencies of circumstances and necessity.

'What shall I do for a living?' she asked aloud, in a dreary monologue. 'End my troubles and difficulties in the river like other homeless ones, or pass onward to the village, and see what fate has in store for me there?'

No, she could not die. The fulness of life in her young body pronounced its veto against the sin of self-destruction. The blood coursing through her veins was highly charged with a vitality so passionate and intense, that the mere physical sense of the enjoyment of the morning air fanning her brow, was sufficient to keep her safe on these slimy, oozy river banks without plung-

ing beneath the stream ; grave, mournful
eyes flitted before her memory ; she saw
that dark-haired man watching her among
the audience, as though a spell drew her
to him.

' I believe if he spoke to me I should
kneel and sob at his feet,' Nellie muttered,
half ashamed of her foolishly sentimental
mood that did not harmonise well with the
hunger attacking her frame.

She possessed no accomplishments that
could be turned to account in respectable
households, but she had picked up smatter-
ings of foreign tongues during their roving
Bohemian encampments ; she had seen gaily-
dressed peasants dance wild Spanish dances
under the shady chestnuts ; she knew the
sound of the Bolero, the music of the casta-
nets ; and with her refined and peculiar
susceptibility, she hated the thought of
service acutely.

Wet and dismal roads, a swampy common,
paths full of briars, tangled. fern, and brush-
wood surrounded her, as she shook back her
loosened hair, and tossed the water over
her burning brow.

Her shoulder still ached and throbbed from
the wound inflicted by the tiger's teeth, but
less painfully than at first, and she had no
fear of Madame Juanita's seeking her out or

compelling her to return ; and at that moment an honest milkman, swinging his cans,
passed by the river, intent on delivering his
morning allowance of milk and cream at the
various houses of the good people of Brooksmere.

Nellie started off at once in pursuit of
him, and touching his arm, said quickly,—

'Could you manage to spare me half-a-
pint of milk ?   I am so faint and worn-out.'

Giving Nellie a mild, bull-like stare, he
merely ejaculated a very vulgar ' Oh, my ! '
doubled himself in half, as if seized with
violent cramp in his stomach, remaining a
moment in this dervish-like attitude ere lifting his head.

In truth, Nellie, with her pale, beautiful
face and feverish-looking eyes — her torn
spangled muslin dress and heavy cloak, all
drenched with the night dew and stained
with river mud, might have brought dis-
ordered fancies before the most reasonable of
God's creatures.

' Lor', child, you've never got a wee bit of
a baby 'idden under that there cloak, 'ave ye,
and been a-tryin' to drown it in the river ? '
he gasped, bringing down his cans with a
fierce clatter on the pathway.

Nellie's look of surprise reassured him,
and she smiled, opening her cloak wide to

convince him that no young head, doomed for destruction, was concealed in her arms.

'But 'ow come ye with that rum gown? A ballet-gal, ain't ye, or sommat o' that sort?'

'Never mind who or what I am,' said Nellie, a little sharply. 'I asked you for a drink of milk. If you don't mean to let me have any—I can buy it of you—why, say so, and—'

'That's the way with you women,' said the milkman, sarcastically. 'If only one man 'as used ye ill, ye fly at all the rest. Of course, ye're welcome to the milk, if ye don't mind drinking out of a little can.'

'What makes you think some man has ill-treated me?' asked Nellie, after a pause, holding the can to be re-filled.

'A pretty lass like you must allays 'ave a lover of some sort. What d'ye say to a biscuit with the milk? Ye seem fairly clammed.'

Nellie seized the biscuit, gratefully offering him sixpence in payment. She shivered a good deal in an odd, convulsive way not lost on the milkman.

'I won't take no money from ye, lass. Strikes me you'll want every penny soon; but I must now be off to my work—families 'ull be a-waiting for their breakfast.'

Nellie thought this man looked kind,

perhaps he might care to listen to her story. She would make one effort to interest him in her welfare.

'Suppose you know that a fellow-creature may be starving for want of food, and that she'd ran away from cruel treatment,' Nellie began, her voice trembling, 'would you let her have some little stray corner in your house to be in for a time, and she'd work hard and eat little, and be grateful—oh, so very, very grateful always?'

Nellie's face kindled as she spoke; some new, yet overmastering dread was conquering her. It was far more terrible to be starving and forsaken out in the world than she had imagined.

The milkman's expression had changed as she pleaded. To be generous to a nondescript kind of beggar in a spangled frock and heavy cloak is one thing; to take that nondescript under your cottage roof, and be exposed yourself to the sharp cross fire of a jealous female's tongue, is another.

'You might not please the missus,' he said shortly, turning away. 'She's mortal particular about her maids' character.'

Nellie shuddered. Was this how they would answer all her appeals?

Some tatters of torn white lace still hung about her bodice and sleeves. Her rose-like breast palpitated with indignation. She wound the rent lace quickly through her fingers, tore it off finally with a jerk, and nearly sobbed.

'He is human,' Nellie muttered. 'Why should I expect miracles or kindness or consideration? I used to wonder once why people thieved and murdered and got put into prison, and died on the gallows. I know now. They suffered and were treated as I shall be—misunderstood and trampled on year after year. How I hate everything human!'

She spoke aloud, and was startled by hearing a soft laugh that made her turn round suddenly, and then run forward with a cry of joy.

'So you hate humanity,' the voice said; 'and what are you doing soliloquising in that theatrical way by a river? Don't be wild and foolish, Nellie.'

'Monsieur Lepelletier, is it really you? Where have you sprung from?'

'You've given me a fine night of it, you wilful little wretch. Patent boots soaked through traversing swamps and puddles, rain trickling down one's back, umbrella blown inside out, all discomforts incurred through searching for you. I meant to have arrived in time to prevent your failure with the tigers, but Ferrara, you must know, was very spiteful. He informed me I was a villain,

and being over-anxious not to be outdone in
telling a lie, I told him he was a gentleman.
He attacked me with a dagger in his hot
Spanish way. I managed to defend myself,
and escaped with a few scratches, arriving
too late to save you, and now I find you
raving like some youthful female *Lear* by a
river.'

'I ran away,' said Nellie, glancing up at
him under her long eyelashes.

'Of course, I knew that. It was the sort
of foolish proceeding to be expected from
such a sprite. You little blind infatuated
mole, what good comes of going to ex-
tremities? Bah! do you live in an age of
Arabian legends? All is real, tough, and
practical enough. Your thin shoes are wet
through. Your hair looks like tow, all that
haze of gold seems washed out of it. Your
cloak is drenched; as for your Hebe-like
arms and shoulders they are perfectly dis-
graceful in their charming nudity. Are you
going to test the tender mercies of some
British matron in that attire? See what she
will say, and yet you expect a respectable
milkman, full of the sanity of remembrances
connected with a pump—you see, I overheard
some of your conversation—to take you into
his employ.'

Nellie's eyes filled.

'Get rid of that sensitiveness, child, if
you have to earn your bread and butter.
Now, what will you do for a living ? Perhaps you anticipate some magnificent proposal from me ? Already in your mind's eye
you may behold some gaily-furnished villa—
a drawing-room *suite* of the best cretonne,
and you richly attired in the latest fashion—
at my expense. You have heard or read
how Miss Lardie Montmorenci drives a pair
of thoroughbreds in the Row, drinks wine—
guinea a bottle port—owns fine diamonds,
and leads some doting, titled imbecile nicely
by the nose. If you look upon me as a
promising victim, please undeceive yourself.'

'You know very well that you don't suspect me of anything of the kind,' said Nellie,
gravely; but she was used to his flights of
speech, and her trustfulness in others, if rudely
shaken, had never been quite dispelled.

It amused M. Lepelletier to tease and
wound her. Of course he meant no harm.
She had not yet learnt to calculate ; she only
trusted.

He took out a delicately-scented handkerchief and shook it in the air.

'Now, here is my proposal, and for the
present, Nellie, I can think of no other
plan for you. I am staying at a romantic

retreat called 'The Lodge,' and with my usual eccentricity, I have a small but neatly furnished room set apart for me; whether with the circus people or polishing my classical tastes, or devoting myself to mesmerism, to this small sanctum do I retire when I choose. Here all the mistakes of my life and the weakness of my intellect are unexposed to public view.'

'Yes; you think too much,' said Nellie, softly.

'The lodge, my sympathetic angel, is inhabited by two estimable and respectable old fogies called Mr and Mrs Faculty Fogg. They are, at least, fifty years behind the age. Beyond driving in a tax-cart to Exeter, and mooning about the Cathedral, or touting for bargains in hosiery, Mrs Faculty has few experiences. Mr Fogg is gardener to some people living in a large mansion called Staplefield Hall. He and his wife, like twin Cerberi at the lodge, guard the gates and the long drive leading to it. The Squire of Brooksmere, Mr Stephen Mallandaine, his wife, and his son, Captain Leonard, all reside at Staplefield Hall — a dismal old place enough, I think, but the family prefer the dismals and go in for clouds and vapours, not the earth and its inhabitants.'

M. Lepelletier's voice had changed since

he mentioned the Mallandaines — emotion
vibrated through it.

Nellie felt surprised and deeply interested.

'And will this gardener and his wife care
to receive me, sir—a lost waif and stray ? '

M. Lepelletier smiled.

'We shall see, Nellie ; we can but try.
I rather think—indeed, I may say I flatter
myself that Faculty will do anything to oblige
me, and Mrs F. is but his echo.'

'And what must I do for the gardener and
his wife ? '

'You will have to sweep their floors, dust
the rooms, peel the potatoes, and occasionally
roast some simple but delicious joint—for
instance, the British leg of mutton on Sunday, served with onion sauce.'

'Then I shall be a servant,' said Nellie
quietly—'with or without wages ; and I hate
service.'

'I perceive the evil spirit of rebellion
again at work in you, Nellie. You must
have no hates, no loves, no anything. You
are an outcast — with luxuriant beauty, I
admit, but a homeless girl ; and don't think
of appearing before the worthy Faculty Fogg
in that *haute école* costume of spangles and
tinsel. Allow me the pleasure of purchasing
you two modest cotton dresses. Let me

cover that golden - brown hair and classic head with the traditional straw bonnet or hat so necessary for the traditionally virtuous young woman seeking her first situation. Let me be the humble friend in lieu of the gay seducer—the champion of honour instead of the plotting libertine.'

'She glanced up at him with a quick and grateful smile.

'How does the programme suit, Nell ?'

'Excellently, sir.'

'Well, then, step out and let us make for the village, so that you shall appear "clothed and in your right mind again." I almost wish I were a painter, Nellie ; I should like to sketch you as you stand at this moment, all tattered and torn ; and the best of you is, that I'm never tempted to fall in love with you ; you are too fragile.'

It was now eight o'clock, a clear and lovely morning. Nellie's spirits revived ; she could even contemplate herself black-leading the gardener's best parlour grate or kitchen stove, or basting a leg of Devonshire mutton with exemplary patience.

'One thing, Nellie, I must warn you about,' the Frenchman said, after a pause, 'is that chapel-going is the chief object of the Foggs' lives ; object to that unseen paradise and you will be lost.'

They were now in the village of Brooksmere, and Baker, the solitary linendraper,
was setting out his little shop to the best
advantage.     He clearly expected a good
order from the well-dressed gentleman, with
his jewel-headed Malacca cane and the
handsome diamond studs and ring.

When the spangled dress had been
changed for the simple cotton garb, and the
hair was roughly plaited under the straw
hat, Lepelletier requested to look at some
cheap black cloth jackets, and Nellie saw
herself very rapidly transformed into a neat,
quiet-looking maiden, very different from the
siren of the circus, with her floating tresses
and sylph-like form in clouds of ærial tulle
and net.

'I often warned you, Nellie, that you
might regret the change,' he said, as if reading her thoughts.    'All will be quiet and
dry-as-dust at the cottage.    You may ultimately find your elective affinity in an
honest yokel.    No lights, no audience, no
horses, no applause ; bedtime at ten, supper
of bread and cheese and cold water—instead
of drunken merriment and noisy sprees.
Choose, Nellie.     There is yet time for
me to take you back to the affectionate
embraces of Madame Juanita.'

'I have chosen,' said Nellie, with one

final survey of herself in the black cloth jacket and thread gloves. ' Take me to the gardener's cottage. I will work for them.'

' Bravo!' he cried. ' I am pleased. Come, Nellie, if you're ready, and I will introduce you to your employers at the lodge, you little golden-haired Peri.'

M. Lepelletier's untiring vitality affected Nellie with no corresponding flow of spirits to-day. She had not yet recovered from the shock of the accident, and how could she look forward to her life at the cottage with pleasure ?

Nellie's girlish thoughts strayed to an unbidden memory, — her first meeting in Regent Street with the man who exercised some unseen yet magnetic influence over her organisation. The grand and rugged brow, the grave, handsome face, with something sweet but melancholy in its expression, like a wearied god's. Why did it haunt her dreams ?

Could a wrecked hope or secret sorrow hold him in bondage ?—and the night previous he looked still more unhappy than at their first meeting. Nellie had ever disdained coarse admiration, but the first physical contact with this unknown stranger in Regent Street, and the curious pitying pain that contact had roused, unconsciously affected her, and stole upon her brain with sensuous, fatal power.

'I hope you'll be happy, Nellie,' Lepelletier said. 'I like you for that substratum of good-breeding and intelligence you possess; but we can only take our goods to market and sell them at the price offered. The worth of anything is just what it will bring. Why, I daresay if poor old Milton had lived in this age, he'd have cultivated his voice and moustache, gone in for the light tenor business, and been more amiable to more wives, or he'd have given over classics to turn his attention to the profitable development of light fiction, and found the prose of railway novels pay better than his immortal verse.'

Nellie felt a little anxious as well as tired as they approached the lodge. It was a pretty-looking rustic cottage, but from its appearance the rooms must be very small and by no means lofty.

She took stock of the windows; monthly roses were placed in crimson pots along the sills, two large cats were purring in the sun, ivy trailed over the pailings, and fine horse-chestnut trees bordered the drive to the hall, and yet Nellie fancied she would regard this quaint spot with the same feeling an eaglet might have for its cage.

'Where's your enthusiasm, Nellie? I expected a volley of admiring exclamations.'

'It seems lonely, sir, and I'm going to strangers.'

'Upon my word, there's no pleasing you, Nellie. I warned you it was not a prospect of Utopian ease and pleasure ; but just take a look at the old hall, embowered in trees, to your right ; that is Squire Mallandaine's home. They are friends of mine.'

He sighed drearily ; it was evident all mention of the Mallandaines fretted his restless nerves.

'Why are those windows to the left all barred and closed like a prison ?' asked Nellie. 'Are the family away from home?'

M. Lepelletier made no reply, and turned the subject hastily. Nellie thought the old mansion had a desolate and neglected look ; it lacked the trimness or display usually bestowed on similar dwellings.

He opened the narrow gate leading to the cottage and startled Mrs Faculty, who was peeling potatoes, by a brisk tap on the window.

'Eh, dearie me, sir, we expected you last night, but Faculty said what with the rain and other things, you couldn't get back in time. He went to chapel, and now I'm getting dinner ready.'

Nellie found herself in one of the tiniest rooms she had ever seen; an old-fashioned clock, belonging to Faculty Fogg's grand-father, appeared afflicted with asthmatical weakness in its works; the books were bound in the fashion of fifty years ago, with the exception of the ' Pilgrim's Progress,' and that choice nursery epic, ' Gulliver's Travels.' There was a bit of rare ' blue ' on a shelf that a connoisseur in old china must have yearned to purchase, a small picture of a soldier after the battle of Malplaquet hung in one corner, facing a young gentleman in velvet, with very long hair and leather shoes; dried grasses were placed on the mantelpiece in real Sèvres vases, and smirk-ing shepherdesses grinned at each other, and at various love-lorn shepherds with crooks in pleasant meadows. An aged and toothless dog, called ' Smut,' looking as if he sadly wanted a severe dose of strychnine, snapped at Nellie—and then gnawed the hearth-rug.

Mrs Fogg was an unusually stout little woman, her neck having long sunk into the regions of her shoulders, like an isthmus swallowed by an ocean; she wore a spotless chemisette folded and refolded over a capa-cious bosom.

' Who's that girl ?' asked Mrs Faculty, not

unkindly, motioning Nellie to a seat, and fanning herself with a duster.

She looked a picture after the good woman's heart, the astute Frenchman having clothed her to the exact taste of the brightest luminary among the 'Winniford Brethren.'

'This young girl will, I hope, be acceptable to you as a helper in your household,' he said, watching her expression.

'Eh, dearie me! but it's what. Faculty will say,' murmured the Echo, *en attendant.*

'Here he is to answer for himself,' said the Frenchman, going to the door; 'and hale and hearty he looks, too, for his age.'

The gardener came slowly along the drive leading from the hall to the lodge, and entered the cottage.

He wore light leather gaiters round his particularly thin legs. A high collar, white cravat, and black suit of clothes gave him the air of a Methodist preacher. He had long passed into a theoretical stage of horticulture, for he merely directed the efforts of the six under-gardeners employed by the squire, playing the tyrant with the quiet enjoyment that all injustice gives to the domineering.

Nellie had risen to her feet at this extraordinary apparition.

'Well, Faculty, how are you?' said Lepelletier. 'You see I've brought the girl I was speaking to you about. Mrs Faculty wants assistance. Now you can both have your breakfasts in bed, and Nellie will wait on you.'

'Ah, sir, you run on so ; it isn't likely we'd begin idle ways at our age,' said Faculty, who took everything *au serieux*, 'and set the young woman a bad example.'

Nellie, who had seen Madame Juanita eat rump-steak and oysters in bed at mid-day, washed down with double stout, wondered what this old man would think of her experiences.

Faculty scrutinised her closely. He could see nothing to displease him in her attire, and the large dark blue eyes were uplifted with an appealing look. Some odd fascination rose from those deep wells peculiarly witching to the masculine intelligence.

'What's your name, young woman ?' Faculty asked severely, determined not to be taken in.

'Nellie Raymond, sir.'

'Do you understand housework ?'

M. Lepelletier's active fingers here spelt 'Yes.'

'Oh, of course, sir,' said Nellie, cheerfully.

'Where have you been employed ?'

There was a pause, in which M. Lepelletier did not come to her aid.

' I have been all my life in a circus.'

Faculty gave a little cry, and the thin legs uncrossed automatically, like a frog's practised on by artificial means as an experiment.

Mrs Faculty's superb bosom quivered like a huge aspic jelly.

' Eh, dearie me ! Used to jumping in and out of tubs and 'oops, and the high falutin' tight-rope business.'

' Silence, wife,' said Faculty, aghast at the Echo's audacity ; ' let me address the young woman.'

' I ask you, as a favour to me,' said M. Lepelletier earnestly, ' to give this young girl a fair trial. She is thoroughly honourable and trustworthy ; she was thrown from babyhood amid a class she hated; she escaped after gross ill-treatment.'

' Nellie Raymond,' said the gardener, ' I am under obligations to this gentleman, and I am willing to oblige him. I have two questions to ask. Do you read your Bible, and do you object to chapel ?'

' I shall be quite willing to go to chapel,' said Nellie, in her sweet submissive way— he fancied tears were in her eyes—' and I read the Bible.'

' Then, Nellie Raymond, I engage you as our helper. As for the members of that evil abode presided over by the arch-fiend—

the Jezebels and infidels of the circus, pray
for them, that they may be rescued from the
everlasting flames.'

The gardener's voice had risen to his
metallic chapel tones; he looked the idealistic
preacher so dear to his hysterical devotees.

'Follow Mrs Faculty; she will show you
the room appointed unto you,' he said, catching a glimpse of the plaited tresses.

'A pretty girl, isn't she?' said the Frenchman, rubbing his hands as Nellie disappeared.

'The heart is deceitful above all things.
We must teach her to eschew evil, for beauty
is a sure bait to the godless,' said Faculty
reproachfully; M. Lepelletier's morals being
terribly lax in the gardener's judgment.

After Mrs Faculty had conducted Nellie
to a room redolent of dried lavender and
camphor scents, and spotless linen sheets
were taken down to be aired, the girl, once
alone, impetuous as ever, and now apparently heartbroken, flung herself down by the
open window, while the leaves of the vine
and clematis flowers shook beneath the grasp
of her hands.

It was a lovely autumn morning. Corn
fields lay to the left, Staplefield Hall and
park were before her, the humming of insects
among the vine leaves, the lowing of cows,

and the deep bay of a hound alone broke the silence.

Her eyes, lit with sombre yet feverish brightness, alighted on the barred windows of the left wing of the mansion.

'I shall be so lonely,' sobbed Nellie ; 'it will be like a prison, and all from seeing that picture in Regent Street setting me against the business— Why did his eyes follow me last night, turning my thoughts, making me wretched, driving me here? I have heard of a glance, a sigh, or frown bringing misery or joy. Who can this man be, I wonder, and shall I ever see him again ?'

# CHAPTER IV.

### THE MYSTERY OF STAPLEFIELD HALL.

AFTER M. Lepelletier left the gardener and his wife, he sauntered leisurely towards Staplefield Hall. It was a large and magnificent building in the Gothic style of architecture, and of a solemn and imposing character. The windows were picturesque; a grand array of old trees, from which rooks cawed and flew, stood out darkly on each side like aged sentinels guarding the lonely old place from ruin. It had a dreary, haunted look; every quaint tale relating to wandering ghosts occurred to the fancy viewing it. It seemed separated from the world as a place peopled by the dead.

And yet its splendour gave it the appearance of being some ducal home rather than one belonging to a Simple squire, but the Mallandaines were reputedly wealthy; they dated their ancestry from Charles the First. Staplefield had belonged to the family for centuries; in many respects it was as historic as Warwick Castle; the picture galleries were crowded with matchless works of art. Paintings by Vandyke, Holbein, Murillo, André del Sarto, besides pictures of the modern school, hung from the noble walls.

Squire Mallandaine was a patron of art. He would write a cheque for a thousand guineas to purchase some rare gem of genius and study with more pleasure and satisfaction than any other outlay could produce.

The hall door was open as M. Lepelletier ascended the steps, and two gentlemen were evidently in deep discussion of some very grave subject of interest. One of these, he perceived, was the family doctor, Mr Chester, the other Captain Mallandaine, the Squire's son and heir.

M. Lepelletier seemed decidedly at home, for, without waiting to be announced, he nodded lightly to the young man and entered the library, where he proceeded to coolly light a cigarette, and taking up the *Quarterly*, turned its pages leisurely over.

The library had a gallery running round it, oak-pannelled and antique; broad terraces jutted out on either side of the mansion, on the edge of which were fine ferns and flowers, and peacocks plumed themselves on the velvet lawns, in the smoothness of which Faculty Fogg and his colleagues took the highest pride.

When M. Lepelletier laid down his book, he saw Leonard Mallandaine approaching from the drawing-room, and the two men shook hands coldly.

'Well, Captain, here I am, just returned from Spain. Any better news of the mysterious and interesting invalid you were telling me of?' he asked lightly. 'I saw the doctor with you just now, and from your very deedy converse together, and your extremely anxious expression, I fear you have scarcely had good news.'

'Our relative is worse to-day,' Captain Mallandaine answered quietly. 'Grave fears are entertained of her living through the night.'

Leonard was tall, pale, and broad-chested, with something ardent and intense in manner and expression, that not all the effects of modern philosophy and cynicism could subdue.

It was a passionate face, for all its sombre gravity, and it bore the shade of anguish. Thoughts were at war with each other, emotion seemed bound and chained; it was a struggle between the natural and the ideal —the senses and the intellect.

'And do you not think in these cases death is often a release?' the mesmerist asked slowly.

Captain Mallandaine shivered a little, and threw himself down in an arm-chair by the side of the Frenchman. Did he shrink from too close and steady a scrutiny?

'What is death? Is it a calamity or a blessing?'

Lepelletier shrugged his shoulders.

'You might as well ask, What is truth? But, candidly, you are in too morbid and *Hamlet*-like a mood. Have we not been friends for years? Did I not love your adorable sister, Aurelia, whom religious craze and superstition drove into a convent to die, making me a visionary and a wreck? And you, Leonard, with youth, wealth, vigour, and every advantage of birth and position, are bent upon eschewing all these, shutting yourself up in a place dull as Locksley Hall, and desolate as a grave.'

'There's no denying it's dull,' Captain Mallandaine answered.

'Duller, too, since this mysterious invalid and relative appeared, eh, Leonard?' asked the other, searchingly. 'Now, what really is the matter with her? Has she a suicidal mania, that you bar the windows? Is there a lunatic hidden in the west wing?'

Captain Mallandaine rose, touching the other's arm.

'I have before asked you to refrain from these questions,' he said reproachfully. 'What is it to you? Say it's sentiment—remorse—affection; that we suffer, you know. There are mysteries and secrets in the dark recesses of many households.'

The Frenchman laughed, a harsh, grating laugh, in which was little pity and less mirth.

'Leonard, I am a mesmerist; I owe you, perhaps, small love for the influence you exercised over your sister Aurelia where I was concerned.'

'You were scarcely fitted for her husband,' the Captain answered, with the faintest mockery in his tones.

'I say I have the power of lifting this veil, of piercing this mystery. If you will once let me look at this person—this victim of hysteria—this pale, phantasmal being, devoured by disease, then I will not bring science or mesmerism to my aid.'

Leonard Mallandaine rose and shook his head. There was a tinge of severity, almost cruel, now in his expression.

'No, Lepelletier, we do not permit you this request.'

'But I insist, in the name of justice—yes, Leonard, and of the law. I demand

that I am once permitted, in the interests of
humanity, to see this person you deliberately shut away from the world; if not—'

The Captain's strong hands clenched together once fiercely, as if he were stifling out
some enemy's life.

'And if not—what then?'

'The law shall either be put in force, or I,
by the aid of mesmerism, will lift the veil.'

'And your motive?' asked Leonard, crushing down his satire. 'I do not appeal to
your gratitude—the memories of years that
unite us—the incessant kindnesses shown to
you from boyhood by my people. Must our
name be bandied in a court of justice, and the
papers rake up every incident of dishonour
that may have darkened our family's annals?
You were fond, you say, of Aurelia—leave us
our clouds and shadows, take your pleasures
like a butterfly.'

'Fond of her! It was adoration. But if,
as you say, Leonard, this invalid is some poor
obscure relative, what is your objection to
my seeing her—I, the friend of the family?'

'She is in a very weak state, refusing food,
sleepless, languid, prostrate. Every kindness
and attention are hers; we pass hours with
her; but any intense mental excitement
might be fatal.'

Lepelletier's face changed; he checked

his next question at the prompting of an after-
thought ; but the look he turned on Leonard
was not pleasant, it had a low and vindictive
meaning.

'Your arguments are all-powerful,' he said
suavely. 'I accept your explanation—as far
as I am concerned, you may cultivate a colony
of lunatics. But, to change this dreary
theme, what kind of a London season has
Timon enjoyed? Much flirting, drinking,
gambling—any follies and delirium?'

'As regards gambling, I hate it, ditto
drinking, flirting most of all.'

'What, are all women objectionable?
Have you no Oriental proclivities for damask
lips and sparkling eyes? Never played the
Grand Mogul, Leonard? You want cheering up. Just the fellow to be seized with the
tender melancholy, and then to say to some
timid *ingénue*, I loved you not, when both
your hearts are beating in unison. At least,
try and fall in love.'

'And find existence embellished by sighs,
dreams, fancies, and jealousy—passion com-
mencing with the illusion trust, to end in
the pitfall marriage.'

The Frenchman laughed again, this time
like a scheming *Mephistopheles*.

'Marriage! But not at all. If you are
hungry, do you rush into a shop and buy

enough joints to last all your life ? No, you take a cutlet, a cake, a cherry, a sandwich, and don't, for gracious sake, be cynical. At your age, you should long with Byron, that womanhood had but one rosy mouth, so that you could embrace splendid variety in one grand unity. Leave cynicism to one who, after copious brandy-drinking and reflection, has discovered that all women are by nature hypocrites—slaves in love, angels in suffering —fair, ineffable, and false.'

' There are times, Lepelletier, when dreams and care—'

' Then you are in love ! Blind mole that I was not to perceive it. Your melancholy and moodiness proclaim it. You are philosophic only in theory—you are intellectual, but you are not wise. I combine the two. I have loved, as you know, your sister Aurelia, far more madly than you, with your British phlegm, could ever love a woman. I plunged into the ideal, the infinite ; I was distracted and sad, but, nevertheless, I reflected, life is short, time passes, age must come, digestion fail, and so I let fair lips, whose pressure brings relief, salute my throbbing brow.'

The Captain lifted his dark and heavy eyes.

' You are a wonderfully practical race, even in your loves, your *cuisine*, your economy,

your amusements, your everything.   Can
you get rid of a little lowness of sentiment,
too?   If *Hamlet* had been a Frenchman,
*Ophelia* would have been his mistress.   You
are not false, but mobile—not fickle, but
playful—not immoral, only philosophic.'
   ' Why do you speak so bitterly ?'
   ' Perhaps I have good reason.'
   ' My dear Leonard, I am trying to reform
you ; spare your metaphysics.   I see a charming young man all women must admire, with
the head and shoulders of a god, a broad and
noble chest.   I know you are splendid, but
you are dying by inches.   I say, therefore,
Fall in love.   Believe me, at your age,
love is necessary to you.'
   The Captain smiled.
   He remembered, perhaps, carelessly enough,
the shy dread, the quivering agony of the
fair wounded girl, whose eyes had opened to
meet his as she lay on some rough straw in
a circus stable—that exquisite golden hue
on hair like burnished wheat, those slender
but rounded limbs, the eyes with deep,
amorous lids and lashes, that shot a mystical
light into his, in spite of her maddening pain ;
he could see the blood streaming over a breast
and shoulder fair as Daphne's ere the laurel
poison darkened their loveliness, the mouth
like a closed blossom—pale and tortured—

that yet, he knew, had tried to smile just once on him.

'Love!' he echoed, after Lepelletier had left, and he was alone. 'To be the slave of some capricious beauty. I can be philosophic as he over the ordinary ills and disappointments of life; but what armour could shield my heart?'

# CHAPTER V.

## CAPTAIN LEONARD MALLANDAINE VISITS THE COTTAGE.

'The desire of the moth for the star,
Of the night for the morrow,
The devotion of something afar
From the sphere of our sorrow.'

WHEN Nellie awoke the following morning at the cottage, she felt wonderfully refreshed after a sound and delicious slumber. The perfumed linen sheets seemed to have embraced and comforted her wearied frame, the pillow encouraged repose, the half-opened window had permitted sweetest air, heavy with the scent of honeysuckles and roses, to enter and play about her temples and tresses and half-bared, warm, white limbs.

She looked fair as some wild flower near a pleasant fountain, fresh as the herb growing by a stream. Her excessive weeping had cleared her brain, and sleep came soothing as the lullaby of the west wind amid pine forests, or as a lover's kisses on the brow of the woman lying on his breast.

It was early when Nellie rose, and, drawing aside the white dimity curtains of the window, looked out at the gardens and lawns of the Hall. Faint wreaths of dew rested on the box-edging and roses, and on the various fruit bushes and cabbages along the borders of Faculty Fogg's cottage garden. Being a servant, she considered it her duty to rise promptly—no sinking again amid the lavender-perfumed bed-clothes, no coy pressure of the pillow with small hands thrown above the golden head in physical enjoyment of the repose of mere sensation.

A smart tap at the door also aroused her. It was M. Lepelletier, who was up earlier than usual.

'Come, Nellie, no idling. Let them see how active my *protégée* can be. The worthy couple are at present snoring as loudly as any member of Circe's herd of swine.'

Nellie laughed. His voice had the friendliness of old acquaintance in it, and something wistful rose to her features that proved how fatally impressionable and sympathetic was her nature ; how soon moved by joy or pain. She was glad her master's metallic tones had not called her on this her first morning of service.

She gathered the golden hair that fell far below her waist in one hand, while she brushed the stray curls off her forehead with the other.

And thus she stood, fair as Vashti, innocent as Esmeralda, passionate as Juliet—a being formed to represent loveliness triumphant over an unjust fate; loveliness to be caressed and prized, to reign supreme over men and women, vanities, luxuries, pleasures, seductions, and yet her lips were cold, her eyes tearful, her heart sad; she was a symbol of all things nameless, homeless, and accursed.

She shook back the hair loosely straying about her shoulders once ere rolling it into the smooth, hard coil which service and slavery demanded, and began that everlasting process of washing and dressing.

The Foggs breakfasted in the kitchen, and Nellie had received orders to prepare the meal in this little white-washed room, set apart for morning prayers and hot coffee, eggs and bacon. After she descended below she saw the Frenchman reading a book on the sofa. He beckoned her towards him.

'Do you believe in ghosts?' he asked, throwing it aside.

Nellie looked both surprised and alarmed.
'Why, sir, is the cottage haunted?'

'Cottage? No. Poverty and ghosts have no connection; the incorporeal spirit has the same preference for mansions as though it were still some golden thorn in the flesh. But look yonder, child.'

Staplefield Hall looked gloomy as ever in the pale morning light. The autumnal haze still enveloped it, it seemed literally buried in mists, the aged trees of the park were conscious of some lazy sense of awakening, for a few leaves fluttered in the wind and fell off, and were slowly carried down the waters of a narrow lake, that also had a stagnant, vitiated look.

'Do you see that place, Nellie—Staplefield Hall?'

'Hardly, sir, as yet, through the heavy mists and trees.'

'Avoid it as if it were a pestilence. It is haunted with ruined hopes, ruined lives, ruined souls. It is the symbol of a world only to be governed and bought by gold. Two years ago I was a poor man—nearly destitute, living from hand to mouth, crouching with the abjectness of some beaten cur, my hand against every man's, and then, Nellie, I cursed Staple field Hall.'

The light had faded out of her face at the passion of his tones. Was she, too, dreading this haunted mansion and its untold secrets and mysteries ?

' But the ghost, sir—is it really haunted ?'

His half-closed eyelids opened, and he smiled sardonically.

' I mean to unveil it to-day, at all events, if one exists.'

' You, sir ?'

She was terrified. Strange beings had at times visited him, of whose conversation and doings she had stood in awe—even Madame Juanita had trembled a little, and said he knew where the dead were, and could talk to spirits of the departed, and even tell her where she had been on certain days.

' Yes, I—by the aid of mesmerism. There may be murder, ay, and madness, under the roof of Staplefield Hall.'

' And the people ?' asked Nellie, amazed at his vehemence, so different from his usual mocking tone.

' The people are— Hush ! I'm going too far. Some day I may tell you the mystery of my life, but take my advice, have nothing to do with any one connected with the place, for they will surely bring you sorrow.'

' You spoke, sir, of a young man—a Captain Leonard, the only son—'

'Of course you'd remember that, or you wouldn't be a woman. Captain Leonard is my enemy—he always was; he objected to my principles and my poverty—bah!—and he says Aurelia died.'

His voice fell away to a whisper.

'Is Captain Mallandaine a wicked young man, sir?'

'What do you mean by wicked, little sprite? He's what the moralist would call, I suppose, a good man; in other words, a hypocrite, most likely. He'll turn up his nose at the face and figure of the finest woman in the world to talk about some ugly little wretch's brow or ardent soul, or humbug of that kind. He's one of your cold, severe critics—cares nothing for burlesque and *opera-bouffe.*'

'I think some people must be descended from monkeys,' said Nellie, drolly, 'because they like antics so, and black their faces and grin and dance like apes, and do absurd things; they hate cleverness, because they are so dull and blind. Perhaps he's too grand for that.'

She was interested in this scornful and god-like soldier, and she dreaded his enemy's malevolence.

'Did you ever see a real, aristocratic love-letter, eh, Nell?' he asked, with one of his quick transitions of mood. 'Look at this magnificent crest—feel the texture of the paper—why, it's worth sixpence a sheet!—and the signature with its bold, characteristic flourish.  Well, I don't mind your seeing it ; it isn't very likely you'll ever meet Laura Branscombe.'

'Indeed, sir, I don't care in the least about it.'

'Come and kiss me this moment, Nellie, like a good, obedient child.  So you don't want to be corrupted by hearing of naughty love-letters ?  I think, though, a man must be a very unsatisfactory sort of a husband if his first wife elopes with an Austrian wine-merchant, and the second is ready to elope with me, having an eye, of course, to my fortune, and the marquisate in perspective.'

'People seem as bad and false in the great world as in a circus,' said Nellie, glad he had not kissed her.

'Get to your work and sweep,' he said cruelly, detecting her aversion.   'Are you not a servant ?  If you give me any airs, I'll walk you off again to the people who pur-chased you.  Sweep as I bid you—to be sure it won't improve your pretty hands.  How Laura would like to copy them for her study of Hebe !  It's a shame such an angel should have to work instead of rejoicing in carriages, flunkies, dresses, gold and silver, and the homage of mankind. Perhaps all these glories may yet be yours. Laura Branscombe's a pretty name, isn't it, and she's a real genius, too?'

'In what, sir, is she a genius?'

'In art—she paints pictures like a man— none of your mock-modest ones; they're hot and cold, and coarse, and refined, and cynical, and classical, and all the rest of it; just like Lollie herself.'

'And this lady loves you. She must be very wicked and unhappy—a traitor to her husband and to you.'

'To me? No, that's the best of it. I'm only her friend. I find her models and draperies, correct her drawing, suggest position, bring her music and gifts, sing her Sicilian songs to a guitar in the twilight, get her the best horses and wines her husband's money can buy, and he's positively grateful, is Branscombe, that I save him worry.'

He laughed, tossing Laura Branscombe's letter on to the table; he then tore it into little pieces, followed Nellie into the kitchen, and threw them into the grate.

'Burn them, Nellie. I'm past the stage of wearing a love-letter next my heart. Thus it is to be rich,' shrugging his shoulders; 'women pester one so.'

'But you said, sir, you were in love.'

'Ah, with an image—a dead image, over whose memory I weep tears bitter as Pygmalion's over his lost goddess, or Petrarch's over his muse.   Why am I heartless and wretched, save through love?'

Nellie had never heard him speak with such fervour.

Would she, too, ever understand this wondrous awakening to another's influence?

'Yes,' she said gently, 'you told me about him.   He was a poet—his sorrow was life-long and real.   Yours mere sentiment, hollow and worthless.'

'Daring and audacious Peri,' he said, his mood suddenly changing.   'Petrarch had, however, his consolation in the joys of a somewhat contracted domestic sphere.   But I must hurry off to London, for I mean to bring an enemy to account.'

Nellie started.   If she could only save this Captain Leonard from his malice.   She felt the same mystical mingling of joy and pain as the peasant Elsie amid the rose gardens felt for Prince Henry, ere she offered up her pure young life in sacrifice for him.

Lepelletier drank off half a tumbler of milk, looked at his watch, kissed Nellie lightly on the brow, and long before the worthy Faculty had descended, was out on the long winding road leading to Brooksmere village.

Once alone the girl sighed. This man horrified her with his gifts, his sorrow, his sorcery. Others had disgusted her; him alone she feared.

She feared also for this unknown Captain Leonard, heir of a noble race. What crime or misery could be concealed behind the desolate walls of the lonely old mansion?

'As if love could ever forget or be concealed,' muttered Nellie, thinking of Petrarch, and then sighed again, remembering Regent Street.

Yes, she saw it all so clearly—the splendid large plate-glass windows of the fashionable picture-dealer's shop. The crowd around it —on one side landscapes, on the other simpering women's faces, at which women stared and men smiled, and then, in the middle, the terrible, ghastly painting of the 'Christian Martyrs,' with blood on the wild animal's fangs, on the fair, mangled girl's body.

She remembered how that choking sensation had risen in her throat—how the sun had burnt her brain—she was so wearied and famished—and then falling on the hard, sun-baked stones of the Regent Street pavement, vanquished by hunger and nervous weakness.

'And now for work,' cried Nellie, looking about for that necessary article, a broom.

The old clock endeavoured to chime six; the dog crept up to her side; she patted his aged head, and flung him a chicken bone in mild propitiation, and leaving him in the kitchen, returned to the little parlour.

Silence everywhere—grave, solemn silence —save that she fancied certain dull snores issued from the bedroom set apart for the conjugal repose of the Foggs.

The morning sky grew rosier as day dawned, the air blew briskly about her brow as she opened the little cottage window.

Her wounded shoulder had ceased throbbing, but Nellie accepted pain as her destiny. It was quite wonderful not to be beaten, bruised, and scorned. Heavens! whose voice was this singing stray fragments of a beautiful air—a mournful, plaintive voice, rich and deep, with which an Apollo or Hermês might have bewitched mankind?

Nellie, looking like some lovely Vashti, turned by mistake into a rustic Cinderella, through the wicked sorcery of a nether sphere, arched her delicate eyebrows, and with suspended breath listened.

'*Mille volte sul campo d'onor,*' sang the voice, always sad, always musical. Never had she heard so rich, so cultivated an expression.

'And yet a person must be happy and have no cares or enemies to dread if they sing,' thought Nellie, in her young ignorance.

The footsteps were coming nearer. Had she some weird prescience who this man was that she hated herself in her prim, cotton dress, linen collar and apron, wishing romantically that she could be applauded before him for risking her life, and looking pretty and smiling in semi-angelic attire.

Nellie opened the window wider, and then crouched on a corner of the sofa, waiting to hear more.

But only a few careless bars of the melody were hummed, and the singer threw himself down on the garden seat under the window, and, taking out a book, began to read.

She could hear him turn the pages rapidly over, and caught the faint reflex of a sigh, and knew that the vines and clematis and passion flowers shook as he carelessly crushed them against the wall.

Fruits were ripening in the morning sun; young rabbits scudded away into the park; monstrous flies and insects hummed and buzzed around; bees and wasps, heavy with the early spoils of fruits and roses, beat

against the window panes ; large yellow
plums rolled off over-ripe on to the warm
mould but a few yards distant from where
he sat within the shade of the passion flower.

Why did Nellie wait and listen ?   What
of her duty to the Foggs ?   The little copper
tea-kettle clearly ought to have been filled,
the fire lighted, the rooms swept.   But
she was a Bohemian, with the brand of
the circus upon her, and no young lioness,
drowsy in the mid-summer heat, ever waited
more carelessly indifferent to the approach
of human beings, amid the long, lush grasses
of the forest than did Nellie at the present
moment.

Her thoughts were filled with an image—
her soul was ruled by a memory, and when
our thoughts are thus concentrated, we are
ever alert, expectant, watchful, although we
may look in vain a thousand times at one
window, or constantly traverse a certain
street, amid careless crowds, seeking the one
we adore.

Nellie listened, governed by a spell, a
physical, almost barbarous instinct, replete
with fancy and bewildering dreams.   In all
tenderness is magnetism, often inspiration.
We dread any thought that may be alien to
or counteract that supreme clinging.   For
this is love's creed.

Nellie had never trembled more in dumb and helpless terror under the lash of the Spaniard than now when this man's voice caught her ear, for he had ceased singing, and was speaking aloud, reading something from a book, and every word seemed to her as if falling from the lips of a god.

Her hands tightened, her breast heaved, all that Lepelletier had told her of Staplefield Hall and its occupants recurred to her, and this man had clearly come from those gloomy portals.

Captain Mallandaine was a bad sleeper; it was his habit to rise early and wander about the grounds and park, and this is what he read aloud, Nellie listening intently to every syllable,—

'For it is the property of crime to extend its mischief over innocence, as it is of virtue to extend its blessings over many that deserve them not, while frequently the author of one or the other is not, as far as we can see, either rewarded or punished.'

He paused here, tossed the hair from his brow as if forming a dauntless resolution, but some struggle full of darkness checked him.

'Heaven help me,' he muttered, 'if my just vengeance has been instrumental in adding to Aurelia's agony!'

'Aurelia! Who could this woman be whose name caused him such keen emotion? Was it some girl he had loved?'

Nellie knew now that the stranger who had come to her assistance amid the crowd on the Regent Street pavement, and who had appeared among the audience at the circus, watching her in the tigers' cage, could be none other than the son of the Squire of Brooksmere—Captain Leonard Mallandaine. And Nellie, with the infatuated folly of girlhood, believed that light and bliss were about to shine on her path.

She could see him from the corner in which she had squeezed herself, with the bloom of the purple passion flowers around him —a strong, dark, stately head thrown back among vines and green leaves, a cold, scornful, passionate face, like a painting by one of the old masters—a beautiful face, lit with the glow of intellect and feeling—a noble nature, and yet devoured by some unseen bitterness.

So entirely centred were his thoughts on one idea, a hidden dread, he seemed to have lost all sympathy with the world. His passions, fiery and strong, were, therefore, locked in or drugged to rest by it. He walked in a world apart, indifferent to all.

It would perhaps have justified Mrs Fogg's predictions of Nellie's future had she seen the girl stealing out at the front door on tiptoe. She wanted to watch Captain Leonard, herself unseen, and from the angle at which she stood she was hidden from his view.

She did not know he had risen as she left the little parlour. They both, therefore, stood face to face by the porch, Nellie longing to beat a rapid retreat indoors again.

Languid and careless, he took in every detail of her luxuriant loveliness, the golden-brown hair, wavy from curliness, about her brow, the flash of pearly teeth between red parted lips, the rise and fall of her bosom, and the quick changing blushes that came and went under his gaze. Then suddenly she turned pale. She forgot she was beautiful, and she knew she was a slave.

Captain Mallandaine recollected where he had last seen her lying wounded in the circus stable, with the dark crimson stain upon her neck and shoulders.

'And how on earth have you found your way here?' he said, smiling. 'A night or two ago you were braving the fury of the wild beasts.'

'It is through you,' said Nellie, passionate under new emotions, and speaking the truth in her ignorance.

He regarded her with amused surprise, her eyes uplifted to his as they had been when the crowd waved before her in Regent Street ; as they had been when her courage failed her in the tigers' cage, and the magnetic power he possessed over her had seemed to give a glory to death, a charm to pain, rapture to despair.

' How am I responsible ? '

' I don't know,' Nellie answered, her eyes burning, ' but— '

' Can you walk a little with me down this path ? ' he asked, smiling again.

He was in the mood to catch at any incident to change monotony, to caress any shy, timid animal that was pleased at his notice, to find solace in the society of any unreasoning human creature.

Nellie obeyed. She could no more resist him than a purple butterfly could help the delicate poise of its wings in the air and sun.

He said gently, — ' You have a history to relate.'

' It was all through Regent Street,' said Nellie, half tearfully.

She knew what that memory had cost her.

' Regent Street ! ' echoed Captain Mallandaine, surprised.

' I had been starved for days, and I ran

away. I crossed many squares and streets. A great thirst seized me. I had a longing to steal, to do something wicked, and be put in prison. It would be an end. I knew if I went back I should be kicked and beaten, and made to work. Some people stood around a large shop. I followed too, and looked, and in looking a great terror seized me. I was starving. The fruits and flowers in the next shop had maddened me with longing for them, but my terror changed all that. Now you understand. Ah, surely you remember ? '

The Captain shook his head. Nellie had clasped her hands, her head bowed.

' I fell down on the hard, hot pavement, and you pushed the people away and came to me, lifted me in your arms, and took me home. I prayed then, and thanked heaven for the first time in my life, and then the other night you looked at me again. I remembered it all. It was a living dread to me, and I ran away—this time never to return.'

He was silent. This clinging, supplicating manner and voice touched him. Perhaps he read something underneath it that did not displease him. It had vibrated through the electric chain of feeling.

' How did you come to Fogg's cottage ? '

'Through Monsieur Lepelletier. He has been good to me.'

Leonard shrugged his shoulders.

'You will hate domestic life?'

'I shall not mind—it will not be so hard if—'

'What was the name of the woman at the circus who rode the " Chesterfield colt ? "'

'Madame Juanita Dalton.'

'Did she ill-treat you?'

'Always.'

He looked at her musingly.

'Nellie Raymond!' cried a harsh metallic voice.

She started, but she feared not. She was too happy now to care what these people might say.

'You will not let them beat or starve me, will you?' she said, gazing up at him with languid joy, and a sense of safety and protection.

'I? My dear child, you are very strange. You had better run in now and do your work.'

'Nellie Raymond,' said the gardener, coming upon them with measured footstep and intent. 'Thou imp of Satan, wherefore art thou not employed? I'll have no circus tricks here, and the daughter of the wanton shall have no home under our roof.'

'Faculty,' said Captain Mallandaine, 'I alone am answerable for this young girl's idleness. I will not have her punished, harassed, or over-worked. Be kind to her. I command it.'

'Ah, but, master, young wenches want a deal of talking to and looking after, and ne'er a room touched nor breakfast seen to—'

The Captain laid his hand on her golden hair.

'Obey him, child, and be patient.'

# CHAPTER VI.

### THE AVENGER OF DISHONOUR.

'I love her though her thoughts are straying
To one who sleeps the dreamless sleep
Of death, though 'mid her sighs are playing
The hopes o'er which her visions weep.'

WHEN the Frenchman left Nellie, and turned his steps in the direction of Brooksmere village, his mind was absorbed with two resolves—to discover the name of the woman concealed behind those barred windows of the west wing of Staplefield Hall, and to ascertain what caused Captain Mallandaine's gloom.

Two years ago the Captain's sister, Aurelia Mallandaine, had been living with her parents and brother at the Hall, when Lepelletier offered her marriage; he was then bitterly poor, she a spirited, dashing girl of rare beauty and brilliant gifts. It was reported a duke had aspired to her hand, and then again, in defiance of her father's wishes, it was stated she had resolved to be an actress; others declared her the authoress of some remarkable poems that had made considerable sensation in literary and artistic circles; then again it was said she had eloped with a sculptor, and lastly came the news that Aurelia Mallandaine was dead.

She was in her nineteenth year when she dismissed her poor suitor with very little compunction. He was, at least, twenty years older than herself; he was poor, eccentric, and obscure. Lepelletier left the Hall in a hot fit of rage, certain that Leonard had indirectly influenced his sister against him, and naturally hating him in consequence, he left Brooksmere, vowing never to return. He travelled, drank, and gambled, nearly died of destitution, but speedily revived on hearing that a large fortune had been left him by a distant relative, of whose existence he had barely ever heard.

Aurelia also went away, and he learnt indirectly that the dashing beauty had changed. She was suffering, so it was given out, from a species of religious melancholia; she was in the hands of priests and nuns; she had given over writing poetry to pen prayers; she fasted and saw visions; she meant to take the veil.

He heard that she ultimately did so ; and
he, in passing afterwards through Italy, was
shown a lonely grave, where they told him
' Sister Aurelia ' was buried, having died of a
fever peculiar to the climate.   The sisters at
the Convent of the Bleeding Heart had wept
bitterly at her mention.

Lepelletier honestly believed this story till
lately, when, returning suddenly to England,
he visited the Mallandaines, and the mystery
of the humble relative suggested thoughts
and fears.

Lepelletier had but few relatives, but there
was one—a distant cousin—a certain Colonel
Oscar de Beriot, in the Hungarian service,
who had been passionately in love with
Aurelia Mallandaine, and Lepelletier had
reason to believe the girl had favoured this
cavalry officer in preference to himself.   Oscar de Beriot was a lawless, mocking, heartless Lothario, the terror of husbands, the
idol of women, the hero of drawing-rooms,
brave as a lion, without conscience, heart, or
honour.   This man had been killed in a duel
on the Belgian frontier, and Lepelletier had
reason to believe Aurelia had withdrawn
into a convent in consequence of his death.
That Oscar de Beriot had met his death
in a duel at the hands of some injured
man, whose honour he had outraged, was

about the most likely end to be expected of him.

Lepelletier had hated Colonel Oscar de Beriot as the poor hate the rich ; the soldier had snubbed his despised cousin, ridiculed him on many occasions, laughing sarcastically at his *beauté mâle.* Lepelletier felt he had now the best of the situation, for he was rich, and Oscar de Beriot had perished at an enemy's hands. What enemy ?

Lepelletier, like most of his race, could console himself with the pastime of love-making in the society of two such antitheses as Madame Juanita, the circus rider, and Laura Branscombe, the perfect and splendid woman of fashion, but his passion for Aurelia Mallandaine had possessed a touch of fanaticism, increased by his own naturally morbid illusions, and he was now by no means sure that the young poetess rested in her convent grave.

As he entered the village, he saw his former enemy, the Cuban, approach. He was dressed in deep mourning, and instead of passing him by with vindictive glances, he uncovered his head and held out his hand.

'We can afford to be friends,' the Cuban said mournfully, his hand on his heart.

' Have you come to request a loan of me ?'

Lepelletier asked, smiling as he tilted his hat on one side.

'Alas, *mon ami!* Have you not heard Juanita is dead?'

'Since when?'

'Since last night. Killed by a fall from the Chesterfield colt. She would ride him bare-backed in defiance of all.'

'Poor Lucrezia! and died in harness after all.'

'She fell on her head, broke an arm, and expired instantly from congestion of the brain.'

'What an end!'

'Shake hands—English fashion,' said the Spaniard, with effusion. 'She was a fine woman. I know she favoured you latterly; she wanted those rare diamonds you once showed her. Dalton had five hundred pounds to marry her, so they say. The poor fellow's quite cut up, and he's talking about Nellie Raymond. He knows something about her history, and he says if she had her rights—'

'Rights be hanged! Wrongs rule the day—besides, she will amuse me by-and-by. Try a cigarette? No? Well, *mon ami*, I'm sorry to hear of your loss. Fate might have spared our Juno; but she made sadly too much flesh lately, and I always thought the Chesterfield colt—he was your gift, you know—would be too much for her. He'd a touch of the wild and savage mustang breed about him, and not all the bits in Christendom can rule them.'

He shook hands with the Cuban, and went on his way. Some doctors would be expecting him about three o'clock at a house in Southampton Row.

He caught an express train, and arrived at the London terminus about half-past one, and after lunching, presented himself at the house where he was expected exactly at the hour arranged. Two bearded, silent, dark-visaged men received him in the hall, and led the way to a room at the back of the house on the second floor, where a young girl, apparently about nineteen years of age, was lying on a couch in a corner near the window. The doctors glanced towards her. She made neither sign nor movement, and had a strange, somnambulistic air.

'Lepelletier,' one of the doctors said slowly, 'this is the second occasion of our meeting. Give me your hand.'

The Frenchman shivered faintly, his eyes fixed on the pallid features of the woman.

His hand glided into the doctor's without further speech, while the spectral features of the sleeper quivered, and, for a moment, a kind of tremor passed over her lips and eyelids.

The other doctor merely watched them indifferently from time to time with the coldness of a Trismegistus.

The man who had addressed Lepelletier took the woman's hand.

'You may ask her any question now, and she will answer,' he said quietly.

Lepelletier had turned deadly pale, his tongue could scarcely form a sentence.

'Who is living in the west wing of Staplefield Hall,' he asked, 'near the village of Brooksmere, Exeter?'

There was a minute's silence; the doctor again bent over her.

'A woman,' the voice answered, clearly and distinctly.

'Describe her.'

'She is young and beautiful; she suffers, and now she prays aloud on her knees. I cannot follow the words; the words are senseless, so also is she. Great grief has brought her to the state in which she now is. There are two people with her; one is her brother.'

'Aurelia, then, lives!' cried Lepelletier in a hoarse voice, 'and it is she!'

'Tell us of her thoughts,' said the doctor.

'Impossible. They are often veiled and shapeless, but there is one name she repeats incessantly—Oscar de Beriot.'

The Frenchman trembled from head to foot, drawing his breath hard.

'The traitor!' he muttered. 'The pitiless traitor! Oscar de Beriot is the cause of Aurelia's anguish.'

'She is praying aloud before a crucifix,' the woman continued, in the same soft tones.

'And what does she say?' he asked breathlessly.

There was a pause, and then the dreamy tones again caught his ear.

'"That is our marriage bell. Do you not hear it, Oscar? To-day is the bridal. Listen to the bells. We will be buried together, dearest. No, no, he comes—the murderer! Leonard, you have killed my lover—you have killed your sister, and he loves me. I must kiss his brow once—just once—and his lips. Oh, my tears! Why am I not dead and quiet in the grave?"'

Lepelletier's terrible presentiment then was true. Oscar de Beriot was a traitor, and Leonard Mallandaine, finding he had forsaken his unhappy sister, had challenged him to a duel and killed him.

It was all horrible, ghastly, and true.

Aurelia, with her instincts of sacrifice, had been the slave of a passion.

'That splendid mind, then, is a wreck ; but I will see her again,' he muttered. 'Leonard shall not dare to keep her thus concealed from my view ; but once—great heaven !—just once to behold her !'

'A sad history,' said the doctor, who had not hitherto spoken.

'It is the story of a good many women's lives,' the other answered.

The somnambulist now arose, the doctor having passed his hand over her brow, and she retired, leaving them alone.

'When a woman has genius, love is often fatal,' the doctor continued ; 'it brings torment. The mind cannot overthrow or conquer its sinister influence.'

'I could have learned to reconcile the thought of her buried in a convent grave,' Lepelletier muttered. 'I could have pictured her as the guileless, innocent saint, penetrated with divine influences in keeping with her purity and refinement. That she has been destroyed, and by him, will impart a spring of bitterness to my every thought. Blessed would have been the sleep of death ; terrible must be the visions of anguish during the vigils of the night.'

He rose, shook hands with the two mysterious doctors, and passed down the stairs into the noisy streets and the light of day.

As he turned the corner of Tottenham Court Road, a magnificent barouche and pair dashed up to the kerbstone, and two ladies bowed most graciously, one with a hot flame on her well-powdered cheek, and the other with a pretty, but studied smile.

The elder of these was Laura Branscombe, the younger her step-daughter Vivian, with a skin of satin, and pale brown hair tightly drawn back off her low, retreating brow.

She was a fashionable beauty, or rather, as she wished to impress on her admirers, a professional beauty, which implied greater distinction and honour ; her eyebrows were faultlessly pencilled, so also were the dark shadows under the lashes.

She had been presented at court by her aunt, Lady Annersley ; her photographs sold at three and sixpence a-piece ; a short review of her life had been given in various papers, the greater part of which was false ; she was described as musical and romantic, when she was more indifferent than intellectual.

All that could be said in her favour was that her head possessed the necessary smallness fashion demanded, that her dark blue riding habit fitted to perfection, and that she rode like a trooper.  She was very tired of everything, and bored by admiration, although she craved it with an appetite sharpened by success.

'So delighted to see you,' Mrs Branscombe cried.  'Of course you'll come to dinner to-night at Prince's Gate ?'

Mrs Branscombe's dress was composed of the richest pompadour silk, trimmed with coquettish little bows, a mantilla of Spanish lace was fastened on one side with a flower, and a duchess hat with saffron-tinted feathers completed her toilet.

The ladies had been shopping, Vivian having taken a fancy to having her boudoir refurnished, choosing pure white panelling, with white gilded furniture.  As an acknowledged belle, Vivian Branscombe was capricious, and her wealthy father indulged her tastes in every way.  Whether buying two guinea bouquets or two hundred guinea thorough-breds, she never thought of the value of money, and in applying belladonna to her eyes, or veloutine to her delicate pearl-like skin, she was always serene and inflexible, seldom enthusiastic, even over millinery.

Lepelletier pressed Laura Branscombe's well-gloved hand lightly as he declined her invitation to dinner.  He was in no mood

for worldliness, he felt morbid and depressed.

'My father was asking to-day after Captain Leonard Mallandaine,' Vivian said, with
the faintest show of interest in her manner.
' Is he well ? '

'He is still devoted to a solitary life,'
Lepelletier answered.

Some one, he was sure, here laughed as
he spoke.  He glanced up quickly and saw
a dark, pock-marked woman seated behind
the ladies with the footman.  She wore a
large black bonnet and cloak ; her face was
veiled, her thin hands beat nervously together.

' Did you not hear a laugh, Miss Branscombe ? ' he asked.

' Get down at once, nurse,' said Vivian
haughtily ; ' go into that shop and ask them
why they have not sent home the sewing
machine I ordered.'

The nurse descended slowly, and the look
she turned on the spoilt beauty Vivian was
not pleasant.  The narrow, serpent-like eyes
gleamed, and then turned dull with pain.

' Old servants are quite too horrid and
dreadful,' said Vivian sharply, so that the
woman could hear.  ' If I'd my way I'd send
her to the union.'

' Oh, would you, my lady, indeed ? ' muttered the nurse to herself, and laughed again, this time quite rudely.

'Mrs Sidewing,' implored the footman, 'do mind your manners. You're getting as fond of liquor as Bob himself.'

Mrs Sidewing scrambled to her feet, choking for breath, and as the footman approached her and touched her arm, she shook him off fiercely.

'I'll have no help, I want nothink o' you, you powdered dandy-loafer! I'll just go back the way I come.'

'Mrs Branscombe, the creature positively defies us,' said Vivian languidly, appealing to her step-mother, and leaning back in her soft laces and grenadine costume of palest rose-colour, her little hands encased in *gris perle* gloves, and her hat of fine white straw, with its trimmings of rose-coloured satin, well over that pearly falsehood—her narrow brow.

Lepelletier was whispering something into Mrs Branscombe's ear; she was too absorbed to listen to Vivian's querulous remarks.

There was a look of fury in the nurse's face, as if some passion, kept down for years by dogged patience, was slowly coursing through her veins.

'Is it only for this,' she muttered brokenly, 'that I have slaved and lied and sinned all these years, and loved her and kept silent?

Ah, to give body and soul, and receive but taunts, and I want to kiss her when I touch her'—shivering—'I want to kneel to her sometimes, and fold her to my heart. Dear heaven, it is cruel to have worked and lived a miserable life only for this all these long years.'

# CHAPTER VII.

## THE FIRST KISS OF LOVE.

' Nothing is more loving than the entreaty of her gaze,
No lily on a tendril more tender than her grace ;
Than he, no one more stricken, such the gloom upon his
    face.'

WHEN Nellie re-entered the cottage, after parting with Captain Mallandaine, she saw her master, Faculty Fogg, take down a gigantic Bible covered with red cloth off a shelf, and gaze at her with the air of a Brutus about to sacrifice his firstborn, as he turned the pages deliberately over. She knew by instinct she should never like her master; his cottage already seemed like a prison, for she had been used to a life of emotion, an unprosaic occupation, with a faint jingling of fame and applause generally going on around her, and Faculty Fogg, with the Ten Commandments written on his iron visage,

petrified her, as a poet might be chilled by
contact with a gravedigger armed with a
practical spade or trowel amid the flowers of
some woodland plain.

Mrs Faculty seemed less objectionable, for
she had addressed some kind words to the
outcast, but as she descended to-day in a
pale slate-coloured gingham morning-robe,
carrying some new laid eggs and raspberries
in a little wicker basket, Nellie saw an
angry glitter in the green eyes, such as an
elderly woman's might reflect who, expecting
a nice, comfortable hot cup of tea, finds
neither fire nor kettle prepared.

'A pretty thing, indeed, Nellie Raymond,'
said her mistress crossly, 'for us to come
down to our breakfast and find you gallivant-
ing about with the Captain.'

There were sundry upheavings and palpi-
tations of that capacious bosom, which the
chapel-goers of Brooksmere regarded in the
light of some handsome if fleshly envelope
enfolding the unseen spiritual loyalty of the
soul.

'I'll have a word with her by-and-by,'
said Faculty, briskly.

'Eh, dearie me, and not even the fire
lighted, or a bit o' wood chopped,' gasped
the Echo, venturing again on an assertion
unprompted by her husband.

'Nellie Raymond,' said Faculty, severely, crossing his legs and addressing the culprit, 'come here. I see you have evil yearnings. I find you have neglected your duties—after supper and slumber, too—under our roof. You, therefore, leave our situation this day week. The godless heathen who brought you hither, may remove you quickly from our sight. Wife, fry me a slice of bread with the bacon ; I think I could relish it.'

'Ah, but, Faculty, give the girl another chance,' said Mrs Fogg, who saw the tears start to the dark blue eyes with their curling lashes.

'I know,' said the gardener, turning over Proverbs with a black-marble expression of countenance, 'that if Nellie Raymond lives with us, I may be tempted to be harsh with her, and endeavour to eradicate the sins, which I can see are too apparent.'

'Oh, sir, let me stay. Give me just another chance,' said Nellie, sobbing outright. 'I'll really work hard, and be a good girl and obedient. I've no home in all the world, no fr—'

'Silence, Nellie Raymond. I look into the future. I see you walking with our young master, the Captain, and I'm a deal too attached to the family to let a pretty young wench get hold over him to give

another stab at his father's heart '—Faculty
here wiped his eyes with a crimson bandana
handkerchief, and Mrs Fogg, looking at the
ceiling, spied a cob-web, which annihilated
sympathy and sentiment as speedily as water
on a bee's wing sends him off a flower—
'and you were talking freely to him, such
as no modest girl would do to a stranger
and a superior; and young men will be
young men.  I shall, therefore, send you
out of the reach of all danger and harm,
for you have beauty of a certain kind.  It's
a snare to the flesh, and a sure temptation
to the senses.'

'Is that my fault?' said Nellie, piteously.
'I can't help being pretty any more than you
can help being ugly.  I'm not a toad, or a
newt, or a lizard,' twisting her cotton apron
into all sort of shapes.

She almost hated her beauty, as something constantly thrown in her teeth as a
reproach.

Faculty started to his feet enraged.

'Go out of our sight!' he roared, flaming
all over.

'Very well, sir, I'll go,' she answered.
''Tisn't likely there would be any kindness in
the world for me.  You can read the Bible,
and send me out of your house, and think
you'll go to heaven all the time.  Why,

thieves and murderers couldn't be harder to a poor girl.'

'You hear her, wife; there's insolence. She's been used to speak her mind and mix with a bad set, the scum of the earth, lawless criminals. We shall next have her setting the place on fire.'

'When am I to leave?' asked Nellie, coldly, checking her sobs.

After all it was a miserable sort of place. To toil and moil here from morning to night would be horrid, and Captain Leonard, fanning her rebellion, had told her she would hate domestic life.

'This day week. In the meantime I'll look about for a place for you. I'm not so harsh and unjust as you think. I'm not going to turn you out to starve. It's for your good I am sending you away. I'll inquire down in the village, or maybe at Exeter to-morrow, and see whether you can be employed.'

'Don't send me far away,' said Nellie, in a dull, low voice, clattering the knives and forks on the kitchen table, and then burning pages of the *Exeter Gazette* in her excitement as she endeavoured to light the fire.

Anywhere near the man with the ivory-pale cheeks and brow, any hopes of seeing him pass to and fro, any chance of a kind word, a look, a smile. Yes, it had already come to this. Nellie felt the keenest interest, an undefinable sympathy in the welfare of the grave soldier with the dark, shadowy hair, command in his eyes, yet oppressed by gloomy scorn. She was in that chrysalid stage of amatory development when a girl does not know what to do with a passion tincturing every thought like invisible poison fumes, or volcanic smoke finding its way unknown into every corner of the heart.

She rushed hurriedly from the room, considerably startling Faculty by her sudden exit. How she hated him, sitting there · so hard and prim and grave ! Nellie was in a curiously vindictive mood. Faculty's great-coat was hanging on a peg behind his bed-room door ; some barbaric instinct made her rush at and slaughter this harmless garment by cutting the lining in several places.

' I'll be as wicked and as bad as ever I can be,' she thought, flinging herself on her little bed in a passion of hysteric sobs. ' Work for him !—no, the old hypocrite, and his poor simpleton of a wife afraid of him, too. They may turn me from their door to-day ; they may kill me, or I'll kill myself. I don't care which.'

She was glad she had cut the coat-lining ;

she wanted the irreproachable Christian to be enraged on Sunday. How angry he would be at chapel—leading with a hymn, too, before addressing the Winneford Brethren—when he found stray flappings of loose lining around him like wings with broken pinions.

There was no breakfast, no work for Nellie to-day; instincts of rebellion were rife within her; she looked out of the ivy-decked casement, beyond the red roses and passion flowers, and saw Captain Mallandaine, the primary cause of her mutiny, standing on the centre lawn with a magnificent deerhound at his feet.

She seized her little straw hat, flew down the corkscrew staircase, nearly breaking her neck in her speed, and ran towards him.

He was rather annoyed this time at Nellie's approach. He was smoking a strong cigar just after having swallowed a cup of *café noir*, and he was reading a letter from Vivian Branscombe, inviting him to join a select party on board her father's yacht, the *Comet*, at a certain time off Southsea.

Vivian's elegantly pointed Italian hand was very agreeable caligraphy, and Vivian herself, cold, fashionable, and uninflammable, charmed him by her very contrast to himself. She was the very last woman living to make

his sorrow hers, or care for his grief, or
enter into his hopes, and yet Leonard liked
to watch the light eyelashes sweep the delicate oval cheek, and feel the *sortilége* of her
soft, satiric speeches, and her strange, careless grace.

The hound started to his feet and growled
as Nellie approached.

'To heel, sir,' said Leonard, angrily,
saluting Eros with his boot, and holding him
by the collar, determined to snub, if necessary,
this very youthful and eccentric helper of the
Foggs.

'He gave me notice,' said Nellie, looking pleadingly into his face, 'because I
spoke to you'—she never called him 'sir,'—
it seemed to her with her tender homage and
reverence, as if he must read and understand
all in the humility of her tones and manner—
'and says I must leave this day week.'

'For what reason?'

He spoke coldly, watching that deep flush
of colour rise under his gaze, and wondering
if the development of the mind and senses of
a little savage beauty might repay him the
trouble.

Leonard was an emotional epicure; he
had, as he declared, no Oriental weaknesses;
flashing eyes, and melting lips, and 'ruinous
lilies in languid hair,' for him had no lure,

but for the patient, striving spirit, the piercing
fancy, the kindly sympathy, he had the keenest admiration ; perhaps he required more
highly strung mental evolutions of rapture
and despair than the ordinary unthinking
sensualist and fool.

And Nellie answered, impetuously—

' Because he said I was pretty. Do you,'
—demurely—' think so, too ? '

Leonard considered this question demanded
quick reproof.

' You have no right to ask any one that,
and even if I thought so, how would it affect
you ? You had better go back to your work
and duties in the cottage.'

' Oh, don't send me away from you so
soon ! ' said Nellie, sobbing again. ' It
can't harm you letting me be with you now
and then, can it ? And it makes me want to
live. If there was anything I could do for
you—if it was in laying down my life to save
you an hour's sorrow, I'd do it. I'm only a
poor, ignorant girl, I know. Be kind to me
a little as you are to your dog.'

Her voice vibrated like chords, and her
face was pale and set. She had something
else to say besides appeal. It was about
himself and his enemy, but speech was very
difficult, since he had turned away his head,
watching the rays of the morning sun alight

on corn fields, park, and woodland till a dusk
flame seemed to warm them anew.

'The man who brought me here is no
friend of yours,' said poor Nellie, trying
to interest him. 'He said'—lowering her
voice, and looking towards the barred windows of the west wing of the gloomy mansion
—"that he would find out who you locked
up there,"' pointing to the house. 'Who is
Aurelia?'

The Captain drew the cigar from his lips.

'Aurelia! And how did you hear that
name?'

'You spoke it aloud as you sat on that
seat by the window, and I listened and heard
it. Is she'—hesitating—'some one you are
fond of, that you shut her away from the
world? I think,' said Nellie, quivering,
'if I loved any one, I'd be jealous of the
very wind that touched their brow, and of
the air they breathed.'

'Is this some romantic simpleton seeking
a hero?' thought the Captain, flinging his
cigar away.

He remembered Vivian Branscombe as
Nellie spoke — Vivian, the heiress and
beauty—cold, passionless, successful Vivian,
who snubbed her step-mother, and ridiculed
her paintings, and got on so well with her
father, Bernard Branscombe, who made a

pet of her, and showered gold on her every caprice.

He intended to marry Vivian some day, if she would have him, and, glancing at the letter she had written him, he did not think there would be much difficulty about that.

Nellie was patting the hound in defiance of both teeth and growls. Vivian would have shaken a three-guinea *point d'Alençon* hand-kerchief scented with ' Parfait Amour,' and requested Eros should be removed or shot, had he evinced similar hostility at her overtures.

' Mind he doesn't bite you,' said the Captain, glancing at her shoulder.

It had been nude and bleeding when he had last seen her, lying in the rough circus stable ; but how fair the skin beneath the crimson stain—how glorious the golden-brown tints of the sunny, flower-wreathed hair! He remembered he had helped to remove a false but glittering necklace from her throat, and it was then the velvet-lidded eyes had opened, and she had tried to smile. Their looks mingled once again, and in mingling they had loved.

But Leonard did not understand this. We often wait hours, days, and weeks to thrill beneath the music of the symphony that fatal prelude announces.

'I'd never care for a dog's bite,' said Nellie, fondling him. 'Once, when I was very little, one of our performing poodles— Marengo, they called him—bit me on the arm; but Jack burnt it all out with a red-hot iron while they held me down.'

'Eros can be very nasty,' said Leonard quietly. 'Don't try him too far.'

'He likes me. He's not savage really. See how he's changing. It was only when you came that night among the audience, and looked at me in a searching way that I felt frightened, and something fluttered in my throat. What was it?'

'After all, she is but a poor, ignorant girl, accustomed to speak her thoughts,' he mused.

The vibrations of her voice were, however, blending with and stirring rare under-currents of feeling, thrilling his senses unconsciously.

'You see me now,' said Nellie, 'in a hideous cotton frock. How could you think me pretty? I wish you could see me in my white muslin dress all spangled, and gold shoes, and my hair undone. Then you might not want to send me away quite so soon, but teach me something about another beautiful sort of life, such as you think of when you are not sad.'

'Nellie,' said Captain Mallandaine, smiling in spite of himself, 'do you so often think of me?'

She pointed to the lake, on which dead leaves were falling one by one, borne along by the stream.

'I thought just now you were like that lake, and I a happy leaf dead on its breast, but so happy, because I was near you. Then again in Regent Street, when you carried me to the cab, I felt a mad longing to thank you and put my arms about your neck— just once; but a sort of dumb trembling stopped me speaking. A long time ago I jumped into the river because I hated my life, and some boatmen took me out; but I never felt glad—only sullen and wretched. There was no joy in finding myself alive— then.'

'I little dreamt of meeting a siren of this description here,' thought Leonard, 'ready to meet me with innocent love in her eyes and voice. She doesn't understand good and evil, right or wrong. No young slave of ancient Rome, no wild witch of Asia, no Helot before her Greek master could be more untutored in civilised ways. Have you ever been to school?' he asked, wondering why he felt elated at her worship.

'Never. I learnt to count through being beaten for falling off the tightrope, and

once, when I had a dreadful fall through
a net breaking, I was laid up ten weeks,
and the doctor came and sat with me, and
lent me books and explained things, and then
an old woman with thin hands came, and
sat and mumbled to herself and talked to me,
and said perhaps she'd come again and take
me away; but we moved on so quickly
from place to place that I never saw her
afterwards.'

' Did no one else instruct you ?'

' Yes, Jack Dalton taught me to write
and read on Sundays when his wife was
tipsy. He never let people be rough to
me, and kept me mostly to the horses.'

' Of course, you ride superbly ? '

' Oh, if you could let me show you how
I can ride,' said Nellie, enthusiastically,
' you might like me better then.'

' Like you better ! My dear child, there
can be no question of liking between us.'

Nellie shuddered. It expressed better
than words the force of the insanity possessing her.

' But if I did you a great service,' she
said, again tearful, ' and saved you from
your enemies, or died for you, would you
quite forget me ? '

He glanced at her warily and incredul-
ously. She amused him as a wanderer

in a desert might welcome some rare
bird with golden plumage, that longed to
hop on his hand and be fed with smiles.
She cared nothing save as he was pleased.

'I never minded when the people hissed
or jeered in the circus, or I got a knock
or a bite; but I do so care,' said Nellie,
touching his arm, 'that you will let me see
you sometimes. I'll go to Exeter and work
in a shop, as they want, but to look into
a thousand faces for long years and never
see yours, why, better be a leaf, a happy
little dead leaf on the lake there.'

'Nellie,' he said, softly, 'why do you
care for me like this?'

'Because you are great and kind, and
you are sad. You hate foolish antics and
fine women who are false and cruel—Monsieur Lepelletier said so. He's quite different. I am very ignorant, but all that seems
clear to me; and why shouldn't I, who
have no home or friends and hate everybody, learn at last to think of one person
as men think of the sun in heaven?'

'Poor child!'

'If I'd been very common, or quite unlike
you, I should have liked stupid dances and
jokes and horrid men, and made hatfuls of
money. They offered me gold to sit for my
portrait, and Jack Dalton wanted to take me

away to live with him ; but no, they told
me I was pretty—that gave me hopes, and
I remembered you.'

Ignorant and barbaric as she was, he
felt implicit faith in her.   Had she been
less innocent she would have locked up
her secret, and adopted artful wiles and
laid her little plots to win him.   A more
vulgar and artful nature must have been
entrapped by greed and gain.

'Nellie,' he said, throwing a pebble into
the waveless waters of the lake, 'I can
trust you.   Tell me what Lepelletier medi-
tated doing against me.'

'He meant to use sorcery—mesmerism
he called it—to find out who the woman
was you had hidden away.   Do you,'
hesitating, 'live alone at the Hall ?'

'At present I am alone.   Would you like
to come and see my home ?   I will take
you through the picture galleries.'

'Like it.   Oh, so much !' she said, with
a little tremulous laugh, and followed him
across the dewy lawns, where the stately
peacocks were pluming themselves in the
sun.

He took her first to the stables.   Three
magnificent thoroughbreds and two hunters,
with dark, glossy coats and fiery eyes, met
their view.   They were faultlessly groomed,

as the shininess of their arched necks testified.

Nellie's face beamed with pleasure. She might be able to show him now that she could do at least brave and daring acts.

In the paroxysms of her weeping, the hard coil had been shaken down, and the golden rain fell in splendid showers about her arms and bust.

Vivian Branscombe, her fortune and fashion, faded out of his mind. Conventionalism did not fascinate at that moment.

'Are these your horses?' she asked passing her little dimpled hand professionally over their sinews.

'Yes, they are. Two are hunters. I send them to the borders of Exmoor when in the mood for a red stag hunt. Exmoor is one of the loveliest spots in Devonshire. The beauties of river, woodland, and cascade are frequently comprehended in one view.'

'Why couldn't I go to Exmoor and hunt too?' she asked, after a pause.

'Nellie, that is naughty. You must never ask such questions. If you are going to be my little friend, you must try and learn something beyond riding.'

'The horses are lovely,' said Nellie, characteristically, and as she spoke she sprang on one like the little wild Arab that she was.

'Mind, he's a brute to kick,' said Captain Mallandaine, feeling the situation ridiculous, for his two grooms, Musgrove and Barney O'Flynn, were looking on and grinning from the harness-room.

Neliie, in her cotton frock and dishevelled hair, rosy, panting, and breathless, seated upon Rosicrucian, that had made his teeth meet last week in Barney's arm, was certainly a strange sight.

Rosicrucian curled back his lip and dropped one ear in a singularly vicious way ere biting the manger and lashing out with his hind-legs.

'Oh, he's a beauty, and isn't he playful?' said Nellie, proud of her feat. 'How we would race the red stag at Exmoor together, and chase him into the river!' she murmured, forgetting the Captain's reproof.

'Is master a-goin' to take up with that there young heathen Chinee, I wonder?' asked the sober-minded coachman, Percival, who had served the family, man and boy, for the last forty years.

'Hofficers are that queer in their ways and whims, they're like so tired, ye see, of grand wimmen, an' ballet gals, drink, an' cards,' said Musgrove, winking at Barney. 'Depend upon it this is some pretty tramp our Captain's picked up off the common.'

'Faith, an' she's a rale beauty intirely,' said Barney, approvingly. 'Only got to dress the child up a bit, and instead o' dancing on that brute's back, why, begorra, she'd make the men dance a pretty tune after her.'

'Get down, Nellie—don't be absurd,' said Leonard, who had overheard some of their remarks.

But at that identical moment, Nellie, flushed, excited, and mischievous, unknown to the Captain, had saddled the thorough-bred, and wheeling him round, galloped out of the stable-yard, leapt a low fence, and was taking him round the park at the speed of a plater.

'Gad! she's off, and no mistake,' said Percival, who had joined the grooms.

'Faith, an' it's sorra a halfporth that Faculty 'ull bless the little vixen,' said Barney, delighted at the scene. 'Shure, she rides like a jockey. 'Deed, an' he'll pack her off pretty quick, for the divil must be in a wench to make the savage baste obey her at all at all.'

The Captain's brow darkened. He was very angry with Nellie. He found admiration for unconventional ways, and beauty had its limits.

'It's the last time she shall ever dare do

that,' he muttered, calling to Eros, who seemed inclined to follow the thoroughbred.

And yet he could not help admiring Nellie's riding, the ease, the grace, the rapidity, and the daring of it all.

She took the viciously-disposed horse three times round the park at full gallop, and then brought him up to the stable door, where the Captain awaited her.

'There, I'm better now,' she said, flinging herself to the ground. 'That was a capital spin, and done him no harm. He wanted it taken out of him.'

The horse's sides were flecked with foam, and he was in that pleasant condition of being what equine critics emphatically call 'blown.'

The grooms grinned at each other, as well they might.

'There's work for you, Barney,' said the coachman. 'He's all of a white lather.'

Leonard did not commence his lecture in the hearing of his servants. He banged the stable door to, again called to the hound, and followed Nellie through the yard to the park.

'Do you know that you have made me ridiculous, and been most disobedient?'

Nellie trembled from head to foot at the tones, but this time no tears came. She was too excited to weep. Her worship and her homage were too over-mastering, and she had so hoped he admired her skill.

'I wanted you to see how I could ride,' she said, timidly, half-turning her head, and pale at his chiding.

'I knew that was among your accomplishments when you came out of a circus,' he said, furiously. 'I was going to take you over the Hall, but you'll be doing some other wild and silly tricks. If you ever ride my horses without permission, I'll never see or speak to you again, or have anything more to do with you.'

Nellie's face had undergone many changes as he spoke. All the light died out of it.

'Was it so wrong?' she asked, piteously. 'Oh, forgive me! I was never taught. Hard words from you I cannot bear. Forgive me. I meant no harm.'

She had clasped his hand unconsciously. Her idol had reproached her.

'You break my heart when you speak so,' said Nellie, shivering all over, and looking like a rose shaken by a winter wind.

She was trying to roll up the ends of her hair with one hand in the hard knot which Mrs Fogg approved of.

'Won't you say you forgive me?' she pleaded. 'I'll never go near the horses or make you angry again.'

So lovely were those fresh young lips

pleading for pardon, so infinite was the grace
of her ways, so entrancing the effect of her
physical beauty, and the alternate charm of
rebukes and humility combined, that Captain
Mallandaine yielded for once to an ungovernable impulse.

He anticipated her yearning for love by a
kiss which thrilled both their lips and hearts
like two worlds approaching, by some magnetic process, nearer together, moved and
warmed by a radiant sun whose burning rays
hasten the oncoming of summer.   And in the
first flush of all passion we can never fathom
the difference between the past and present states of feeling when there exists the
memory of a kiss.

# CHAPTER VIII.

### THE LOSS OF A DIAMOND NECKLACE.

VIVIAN BRANSCOMBE is sitting before the lace-decked mirror in her dressing-room, her chin buried in her hands, apparently oppressed with thought. Is the spoilt belle in love? Has the favoured 'beauty-woman' found some careless lover disdainful of her charms? Has all the gold showered upon her from her extreme youth brought mere weariness and vexation of spirit? Can there be a limit to the enjoyment of dressing, riding, and flirting? Her exquisite shoes of fine kid, buttoned at the side according to the latest fashion, have been kicked off in sudden disgust and *ennui*, and when a beauty's restless feet deal havoc to her shoes, we may be sure that floods of tears or furious words, or the frantic perversity of the spoilt child of wealth and fashion, are about to culminate in some tremendous anti-climax.

'Leonard has never answered my note,' Vivian murmured, driving her silken-covered foot again into the despised shoe. 'Why does he keep away from me, and shut himself up in Staplefield Hall? I almost wish there would be a war, and then we could read an account of his bravery in action.'

'Shall I dress your hair, miss, for your ride?' asked the lady's-maid, Morton, respectfully, her young lady's tantrums being clearly revealed to her astute observation.

'I don't know,' answered Vivian, abstractedly, and sighing.

'If you please, miss, a gentleman begged me to leave this for you to look at,' said Morton, who had pocketed a sovereign by the transaction. 'He waylaid me as I was crossing the road, and he says, "Do you come from that angel, the beautiful Miss Branscombe?"'

'So ridiculous,' muttered Vivian, looking, however, delighted, and sparing the other shoe.

'And I says, "Yes, sir, I'm her maid." Then, says he, "Give her this, and tell her one as watched her last night from her box in the theatre, and dreams of her by night and by day, begs—"'

'Oh, how many more, I wonder?' the beauty cried, stretching her lovely arms above her head. 'The fellow's a pickpocket, I daresay. These adventurers are always on the look-out for something to turn up to their advantage. What is it—a begging letter, a likeness, or some idiotic poetry?'

Vivian opened a crumpled envelope, and read these lines :—

'Alfred de Lancy entreats the favour of an interview with the beautiful Miss Branscombe. He played the part of *Claude Melnotte* when she visited the Prince's, and is ravished with the memory of his charmer's eyes. He feels that Miss Branscombe must be either his death or destiny. If he could only be a servant in her household, even a footman, or groom—'

'Here, Morton, that's more than enough,' said Vivian, laughing. 'The very idea of such insolence! Groom, indeed! He'd better not try any nonsense on of that kind, or I'll have him horsewhipped.'

She put the letter in a box on her dressing-table, and thought no more of the matter. Morton also pocketed de Lancy's sovereign, and meant to appropriate more.

Vivian's step-mother, Mrs Branscombe, writing letters in the library, and Bernard Branscombe, busy in his study, signing contracts, settling mortgages, and buying up old country mansions long gone to rack and ruin, were hardly what the moralist would call choice specimens of the model couple so sweetly embodied in that charming ballad, ' John Anderson my Jo.'

The Branscombes were still at Prince's Gate, though the London season had long ended, but they intended yachting very shortly, and the ladies evinced no particular desire to retire to Bernard Branscombe's fine old country seat, Beechwood Manor.

Vivian flung open her wardrobe door, and selected the newest riding-habit she possessed ; it was splendidly finished by a West-end tailor, and was composed of the finest, darkest blue cloth. All the snobs and toadies of Vivian's acquaintance, and various young idiots of good birth and no money, having an eye to Branscombe's gold, paid the spoilt heiress that exaggerated homage which only accompanies the promptings of self-interest.

Branscombe's faculty for money getting and Vivian's hauteur and beauty formed a safe and amusing topic for the toadies, and whether Vivian were lolling indolently back in her father's carriage or flashing past them in the Row on her dark chesnut mare, there were plenty of admiring ' by Joves ' and ' by Georges,' and ' ohs ' and ' ahs,' which Vivian regarded no more than the Princess of Wales might pause to consider the value of mince-meat for the Christmas pies.

As the heiress lifted her riding-habit some impulse made her open her Coromandel wood dressing-case, and taking a small gold key attached to her chain, she opened the box and ran her eye carelessly over the jewels.

Presently she started and hastily turned the gems out on her dressing-table. A very fine and valuable diamond necklace of small but rare rose diamonds was missing.

A curious tremor seized the girl; it seemed as if a spectre had laid its icy grip upon her. Vivian was not constitutionally nervous—quite the contrary—but she had a prescience of coming ill, of something unsound and dangerous about her path, connected with the loss of the diamond necklace. She uttered a low, smothered cry of fear, and her face had an ashy pallor, not from a sense of loss, but from a hidden and impending dread.

'Morton,' cried Vivian, imperiously, 'you remember my diamond necklace—the one I always wore with my violet and white velvet dinner dresses—well, it's gone; no mistake about that.'

She flew downstairs and rushed into the study in which Bernard Branscombe, her father, sat among his deeds and papers, in company with Mr Warrington, the family lawyer.

'My dear Vivian,' said her father, motioning her to a chair, 'whatever is the matter? My nerves never could stand the banging of doors.'

Bernard Branscombe was a very small and slender man, with a thin, keen face, an aquiline nose, and small, shifting, pale blue eyes. Why he was so rich must have astonished any physiologist or phrenologist regarding his organs and faculties, but is it mind that is necessary in getting on? Decidedly not. Given lucky chances, gross unscrupulousness, and no feeling or imagination, and the successful soap-boiler, contractor, or merchant will coin wealth like others of his kind in a world which makes money without pleasure to itself.

His little blue eyes seem to open and shut, and retreat back again into his head like those of a sleepy alligator. An honest citizen, a thorough man of business, always in a hurry in his office, and fond of charging columns of closed envelopes with a paper knife, he was decidedly not a pleasant man, nor one to be taken too familiarly by the hand.

'Papa,' cried Vivian, forgetting to salute the lawyer, 'only think, my diamond necklace has gone.'

Then she stopped. She had been pale when she entered, but now the colour darted all over her face with rage.

'The rose-diamonds gone?' said Bernard Branscombe, adding up some interest. 'Why, they were my wedding gift to your mother, Vivian, when she was Emily Gregson, and before she did me the honour to elope with my bosom friend, Hubert Rudersheim.'

'I hate to hear of my mother's name,' said Vivian, savagely; 'it enrages me. Think, papa, how she disgraced us.'

'Pardon me, my dear Miss Branscombe,' said the lawyer, taking up cudgels on behalf of the absent lady. 'Your mother is now very happily married to Mr Hubert Rudersheim, and I don't like to hear her traduced by her daughter.'

'Did she care what became of me?' said Vivian, passionately. 'Did she not forsake me soon after I was born, and leave me to the care of strangers?'

'Emily had no maternal instincts,' murmured the forsaken spouse, who had long consoled himself.

'If it had not been for my dear father's goodness in sending for and adopting me, and reinstating me in my true position as his heiress, I should have drifted on the world a creature of chance. I don't forget that I was born pending the separation and divorce of my mother and Mr Branscombe, and that she left me to the tender mercies of miserable mendicants.'

'Emily was always thoughtless and selfish,' said Mr Branscombe, wearily; 'yes, and weak, I don't know why all women should strike me in that light. And why did I send for our child? Because I found my second wife Laura as incompatible with me in her tastes and disposition as my first.'

'You are singularly unlike your mother,' the lawyer said thoughtfully, addressing Vivian, 'she was weak and yielding to a fault, but she spoke kindly even of her enemies; she always tried to repair any injury she had worked. There'—pointing to a large oil-painting over which was hung a velvet curtain, which he drew aside—'is the ideal portrait of Emily Gregson in all her youth and loveliness ere your father married her. Look at the sweetness of the lines of the mouth, the satin-lidded eyes, the arched brows, the golden hair! Tell me, Branscombe, did you ever see eyes with so dark and lovely a shade of blue?'

'Yes, Emily was very beautiful,' calmly replied the husband who had lost her.

'I'm very glad, indeed, I don't resemble my mother,' said Vivian haughtily. 'There was nothing to admire in her conduct, not even in a worldly point of view. But now, papa, we won't rake up stale dead and gone memories,' re-covering the portrait. 'It's about my diamond necklace—it's gone to a certainty, and some one must have stolen it.'

'Stolen it!' echoed both men, in a breath.

'Oh, nonsense, Vivian,' said her father. 'You've mislaid it, my dear, and will find it in some corner of your room.'

'I tell you, papa, I've long had reasons to suspect the woman you have such implicit confidence in. Nurse Sidewing defies me to my face, and drinks terribly, all the servants say. She and her wretched husband have no right to be encouraged in our household.'

'But I'm partial to old servants,' said Mr Branscombe, quietly. 'She knew the people at the house your mother fled to, and where you were born. For a long time I resolved never to see you, but I must do Mrs Sidewing the justice to say she left no stone unturned to reinstate you in your proper position under my roof.'

'But now, papa, about my necklace. I've a strong suspicion Sidewing has stolen it, and, if so, you will not spare her because she is simply an old servant. You will let justice be done and make an example of her?'

Mr Branscombe looked uncomfortable.

'I hope there will be no need of anything of the kind,' he said; 'but suppose, my dear, you ring the bell and order Mrs Sidewing to come to us here.'

At this moment Laura Branscombe, wearing a rich gros-grain black silk with robings of pale blue satin, glided softly into the room.

She was a magnificent-looking woman between thirty-eight and thirty-nine years of age, her complexion that of a clear brunette, her hair blue-black and drawn off a wide, low brow.

An air of sadness, but one of resolute and dauntless spirit and determination, was reflected in the lustrous brilliancy of her dark eyes; she suggested the idea of a woman of genius, whose life was broken or incomplete.

Laura Branscombe had none of the splendid ingratitude, the cold sensuality, the selfish forgetfulness of a woman of a merely fashionable circle; she had a man's talent with her sex's fatal weakness of organisation, hence the struggle of her life.

'Laura,' said her husband, in an acrid voice, in which, however, was command, 'how was it you came home so late last night after all the household had retired to rest? Although my room is at the back of the house, I heard you come up the stairs.'

Vivian smiled, glancing at the lawyer.

'Does Mr Branscombe desire to know where I was last night?' asked Laura, with an abstracted look. 'At my sister's, in Grosvenor Square. Some young people looked in, and somehow we knocked up a little dance. She sent me home after in her carriage. It was a nice change.'

'Were you alone?'

'Mr Branscombe, I did not come here to be cross-questioned in this way,' said Laura, angrily, her large brows darkening. 'No, I was not alone.'

Mr Warrington looked grave. He had often pitied the passionate, beautiful woman tied to this little cold, dry-as-dust man of business, who ought to have married a very mild 'Rosa Matilda' sort of person with the average pretty female feebleness.

'And who had the honour of bringing my wife to my door at three in the morning— London, remember, is not Rome or Naples— but the charming Frenchman, my friend Lepelletier? I heard the leave-taking, it was worthy of French comedy—the kiss on the extended ungloved hand, the tender *ma chere*, the smothered reproof. I know I'm not a too careful or jealous husband, but one objects to this sort of thing, you know; it's past all bearing when one's wife is brought home by her lover.'

'So you dare at last to insult me, and before them, too,' said Laura, coming a step forward.

'Lepelletier will be Marquis de Rocheville some day,' said Mr Branscombe, coolly. 'He's an utter scamp, always remember that —a man of words, morbid, because soaked in absinthe, noisy, heartless, and selfish to the core, and in the sere and yellow leaf of age, such men are worse than in their hot youth.'

Mr Branscombe was not quite a dullard; he might have been so unlucky as always to marry the wrong woman, but he could estimate high-sounding commonplaces at their just value.

Laura had sunk into almost pathetic silence.

The lawyer lifted his hands in mild protest. The family trials of the Branscombes had already put many pounds into his pocket. He now sees in the future a probable scandal, and in the present a brisk conjugal passage of arms.

'When I married you from off the stage, Laura, in defiance of the advice of all my friends, it was part of your trade to assume any part. I was warned you were extravagant'—Mr Branscombe shuddered—'still extravagance does not affect me, but why

will you persevere in acting still ?   One of
these days your social play will have a sorry
ending.   Spare me in the meantime any
domestic melodrama, or else leave my house
altogether.'

Laura's blue-black hair contrasted strangely
with her pallor.   She griped the back of a
chair for support, her bosom heaved.   The
lawyer darted forward, and, seizing a bottle
of Vivian's smelling salts, offered them to
Mrs Branscombe with a few kind words.

It was a painful scene ; it somehow excited
his compassion.

' Must I pay the price,' he heard her gasp,
' or forget Gustave ? '

Burning tears were in her eyes, a sort of
feverish rage seized her ; he thought of
Phædra as she swept from the room.

' A valuable helpmate,' said Mr Branscombe, with unpleasant irony, his little eyes
retreating into their sunken orbits ; ' there's
conjugal sympathy and affection ! '

' You are unlucky in the selection of your
wives, my dear Branscombe,' the lawyer
said gravely.   ' Mrs Branscombe is a clever
woman—I almost said a woman of genius ;
her paintings deserve to be immortalised.
You wanted a homely fool, a pleasant,
common-place person, too dull to doubt anything.'

'All artists are peculiar,' said Vivian; 'they are so exacting, and expect such a fuss made about them.'

'If Lepelletier has turned her head—he's one of your fast Parisian scoffers, a gambler, and a duellist into the bargain—Laura will be ready for any madness, and when her pride becomes secondary—Oh, yes, my dear Warrington, you'll have plenty more work with us besides mortgages and contracts. And now let us see about Vivian's loss of her diamond necklace.'

Vivian rang the bell sharply, and it was speedily answered by the young footman Joyce.

'Say we desire to see Mrs Sidewing at once,' Vivian said, shaking the laces on her sleeve.

Joyce was absent a few minutes, and then returned, looking graver than before.

'If you please, miss, nurse Sidewing refuses to come.'

'Ah, Vivian, you and that woman never did get on well together. Humour her, my dear child, humour her by all means,' said Mr Branscombe, anxious for peace.

'I hate her,' said Vivian, vindictively; 'and if I find it is she who has stolen my necklace, may I not have the matter looked into, and give the thief in charge of a policeman!'

'We could not permit dishonesty among our servants, but I fancy, Vivian, if your diamond necklace has gone, you will have to look further a-field for it.'

Vivian meanwhile left the room, and descended into the servants' hall.

She found the nurse knitting a pair of woollen stockings, and partaking of a lunch of bread and cheese.

'You refused to obey my orders,' said Vivian, haughtily.

Mrs Sidewing moved her head so suddenly that her heavy black lace cap rolled sideways. She seemed half-dazed as Vivian spoke.

She still kept her eyes fixed on Vivian, and as she looked, that former catching of the breath paralysed her speech, and the thin hands began their old nervous trick of beating restlessly together.

'Oh, yes, I hear you,' she said, seizing her knitting-pins.

'Are you aware that my diamond necklace is missing?' asked Vivian, coming a step nearer.

The servants all started, and glanced from one to the other.

'Missing, is it? Well, I daresay it 'ull be found again soon,' said the nurse, with the scant courtesy she usually gave her young mistress.

' Is that the way you speak to me ?' cried Vivian, losing all self-control. ' Do you know that I have my father's permission to track and punish the thief who has stolen my necklace ? I know it is stolen '—she paused, with her usual self-satisfied air,—' and I shall most certainly send Joyce with a note to the chief inspector at Scotland Yard, and ask him to step up and make inquiries and investigations here.'

As Vivian named Scotland Yard, Mrs Sidewing had shifted her former position. Crimes and mysteries were as familiar to the clear-sighted officials there represented as audacious romances to French dramatists.

The woman had by this time shuffled on to her feet, and put her hands before her eyes.

' Come here, miss, a minute, will you, please ?' Mrs Sidewing said, moving quietly away from the servants' hall. ' I want a word or two with you as private as possible.'

There was now a look in her eyes that Vivian had never remarked before, and which literally frightened her. How can we account for that sudden flash of instinctive terror, unrevealed, save through the medium of expression ?

Mrs Sidewing understood she was getting a mental mastery over Vivian, and smiled.

All the girl's grand airs of assumption and superiority faded, and she actually followed the nurse meekly out of the servants' hall into the sumptuously furnished dining-room, with its dark crimson curtains, its panelled walls, and rich velvet furniture.

Mrs Sidewing seated herself very composedly on the crimson velvet couch, and then the threatening look again darted from her eyes.

'She's a coward, after all, like him,' she muttered, so low that Vivian could not catch the words.

'I've borne your insults a long time,' said Mrs Sidewing, wearily, and calculating the effect of every tone. 'Please remember this. Well, then, I tell you to mind what you're about, for I'm like a snake that can—' Vivian stared at her in dead silence, her heart beating strangely, but there was more to hear. 'A snake with poison, as 'ull be the ruin of you and your grandeur, and your hopes, as sure as ever you come the policeman dodge over me.'

'Oh heaven! what do you mean?' cried Vivian, trembling all over.

'And then, where's your fine lover Captain Mallandaine's promises, and where's all your friends as dances about you as if you were a queen?'

" I repeat, what would you imply ? ' murmured Vivian, trying to keep her mind perfectly clear.

'What I says. No more nor less. Leave me alone ; don't flourish your nonsense over my 'ead afore the servants, and master, and missus, and I'll leave you alone. I've been kind to you. I was fond of you, but you've a black, bad, bitter 'eart, my dear, and some day, miss—oh, my 'ead, 'ow it do throb—that there snake-like nature in me 'ull get the better of me, and I'll be sorry after, but I shall spring and strike you down.'

Vivian had ceased trembling. She knew there was danger—an awful, invisible, and yet tangible danger known only to this terrible old woman, towards whom she had been always so hard and merciless.

Mrs Sidewing started to her feet, and rushing over to Vivian, threw herself sobbing by her side.

'Oh, dearie, dearie, a little love, a little kindness, for pity's sake ! Oh, my dear, I'll not 'arm a 'air of yer 'ead ! I'm so ill and weak, an' he's a bad 'usband to me, is Bob. He's got a cruel 'eart, an' a bitter tongue ; and a bad 'usband is a trial, miss, ain't it ? '

'You must be mad, nurse Sidewing,' said Vivian, trembling again.

The existence of some fearful and destructive secret unknown to her, and which yet might blight her life and hopes, had been revealed in that lightning flash of passion in the woman's words, and Vivian was at heart a coward.

She had a peevish sense of injury and anger, but she would like the curtain folded well over the secret, and not force the hand of destiny in removing it.

'I must smooth her down, and keep my temper,' the heiress reflected.

All her swaggering manner had gone ; she was cowed and overawed.

' Nurse, did you really take the necklace ? ' said Vivian, prepared to let her keep it, and send for no policeman, sooner than again hear those fearful threats.

' No, dearie—I took no necklace. Why can't you say a kind word to your poor old nurse as cared for you when you was a little 'un ? '

A new terror seized Vivian. Something in the woman's manner and tones, allied with her past warnings, had brought a fresh train of thought and suspicions.

' Nurse,' said Vivian, lifting her hands to her brows, 'am I really like my mother—like that blue - eyed simpering doll in the old painting ? '

The nurse's thoughts wandered to the

memory of a sick young child, with a broken arm, and dark, lustreless, wan eyes, uplifted entreatingly for love—a child that shivered at the harsh tones in which it was addressed, and that had cried through weary nights, praying to die.

'No, my dear — you're not like your mother. She left you in the care of an old woman at Exeter, and paid her a good sum to take care of you ; and then I talked to your father, and he quarrelled with Madam Laura—she's got the temper of a dozen fiends —and he sent me to find you, so as to spite Madam Laura, and made you his heiress. I went to Exeter'—her face here changed again and quivered—'and I brought you back to your father's roof.'

'Nurse,' said Vivian, pale again, 'I was wrong to be so unkind to you, but I never quite understood how — how good you've been to me, nor how bad it was of my mother to forsake me.'

'And you'll leave poor nurse Sidewing alone in future, dearie, won't you, and not want to send her to gaol ? And here's Bob, I do declare, a-staggerin' at the area gate, and over he'll be and no mistake, for he's as drunk as a lord, as the sayin' goes.'

Mrs Sidewing darted after her objectionable husband—a gentleman who invariably levied black - mail whenever he found a chance—and drew him into a little room adjoining the kitchen.

Bob was a drunken actor whom Mrs Sidewing — then Martha Appleby — had fallen deeply in love with years ago and had married, prior to the occasion of some festivities given on the return of Mr Branscombe and his second wife, Laura, to Beechwood Manor.

'Well, wife,' said Bob, throwing a limp tie on the table, 'I am as usual in want of money, and money I'll have, or I'll find out where our girl is, or what she died of.'

Mrs Sidewing felt in her pocket, and ultimately produced a brown leather purse, out of which she deposited ten sovereigns.

'Capital! Quids, and good 'uns, I'll be bound!'

He spun a sovereign in the air.

'Don't ye want to know 'ow I got 'em, Bob? Oh, my 'ead! It'll burst one of these days.'

'I never ask impertinent questions of ladies,' said Bob, slyly. 'Don't you want to know how yours truly has been getting along? Models have a hard life. I've sat for five cavaliers, Martha—one combing his hair, another on a pair of high steps, the others mostly military parties preparing for a charge.'

'You've never done a proper day's work for years.'

Bob threw himself into a telling attitude.

'When our little girl was born you were only Martha Appleby. You were a good ten years older than me, and uncommon loving. Don't forget I made an honest woman of you afterwards; and now get me some beer.'

'And why did you marry me? Because of the thousand pounds from master, never to let his bride 'ear of that child born at Exeter afore the divorce, but after, when they quarrelled, he was very glad to adopt her; and she's a real beauty, is Miss Vivian.'

Bob snapped his fingers in his wife's face.

'It was never very clear to me, my dear, how you got rid of our little daughter,' said Bob, looking at the money—'no, nor where she was buried, nor what she died of; but as long as you pay me I'll not rake up by-gones; but I sometimes think our little 'un did not die, and that you may have changed the children—you're bad enough for any-thing — and that her they call Nellie Ray—'

'Hush!' cried Mrs Sidewing, starting up. 'I thought I heard a cry.'

A pale, horrified girl had listened — a

shrinking form staggered backwards as these words were uttered.

'Can she have stolen the diamond necklace to pay him?' muttered Vivian, a light breaking in on her.

And with a piercing shriek, she fell senseless to the ground.

# CHAPTER IX.

## NELLIE'S POSITION IMPROVES.

> ' Know you not
> Such touches are but embassies of love?'

CAPTAIN MALLANDAINE declared to himself that Nellie was pretty; he may even have gone further, and used the latest modern phrase of drawing-room slang to express his feeling, 'quite too awfully pretty,' as she reddened in surprised delight after that dangerous kiss.

'But never again,' muttered this son of Mars, shaking his dark head. Men, when they first begin to tumble over head and ears in love, always say 'never again,' in recalling some fatal amatory skirmish. 'Never will I give another chance to the enemy of our souls in leading us both neatly to perdition.'

Easier to stop Ixion's wheel than the multitudinous fancies of love. Like a man

who sees rare and golden fruit ready for his
hand to gather, but to grasp which he must
needs wade through dark and sodden pools,
so the Captain resolved to close his eyes and
heart against the fatal fascinations of this
half-gipsy girl, unlike other gipsies, however,
in the fair, Greuze-like tints of her complexion.

He saw ' Danger' written in capital letters ;
' Rocks Ahead' of an alarming character, and
one never exactly knows what form or di-
mensions temptation and mischief will take
after that first indefinable sympathy has been
aroused between two of an opposite sex, on
a bright autumn morning, with delicious
wall fruit ripening in a mild sun, and a
thousand fragrant scents wafted around by a
pleasant south-west wind.

Especially, too, when a pretty little
simpleton, who doesn't know what it is to be
heartless, lifts big blue eyes, shaded in with
dark curling lashes, like a Venetian beauty,
and seems to beg to be petted like a kitten—
an adorable little simpleton, anxious to tell
you, quite innocently, of course, after perhaps a few more interviews of a like agreeable character, that she thinks a person ought
to be ready to sacrifice body and soul, if
necessary, for the sake of an earthly love.

' By Jove ! she's what one would call

*intense,* I suppose,' he thought walking slowly towards the home of his ancestors. ' Case of ignorance and intensity combined, watching Nellie's little heels peeping in and out under her cotton gown as she rushed along the path back again to the cottage.'

The Captain was not unacquainted with splendid ladies of rank and fashion, attired in the latest æsthetic costumes or duchesse hats ; women of a very different world and stamp to the *divas* of South Belgravia and St John's Wood, and yet who were anxious to ' out-Herod ' these in eccentricity of dress, luxury, and display. He understood women fairly well, not with the exquisite subtlety and platonic grace of a Balzac, but with more than the careless analysis of the ordinary man of the world. He could unveil love's hypocrisies, and knew when fair lids drooped from passion or coquetry, and when alabaster necks rose and fell from emotion or design. But he had never met with a perfect, all-absorbing devotion.

' Darling little dunce !' he mused. ' I daresay she's never learnt the catechism, or looked at a fashion-plate, or even wondered how she should dress her back hair. She's natural as Eve in the garden of Eden before the serpent—in other words, the world—set her teeth on edge with the apple.'

The Captain's recollections of Regent Street, its handsome shops, its elderly *habitués* and various young members of the upper ten, its wickedness, assignations, and *demi-monde* were not of the embarrassing nature attending many men's. Regent Street was now to him the centre of a romantic train of thoughts, and already a certain gloom seemed lifted from his spirits ; a street pre-eminent in vice, had yet brought romance to him in which faint mystical pain and longing mingled.

He had been generous, brave, and un-selfish; he had avenged a beloved and injured sister's honour ; he had become a soldier instead of a *littérateur* loving the shadowy dreamland of thought and fantastic idealism —to please the proud and aged father, who was so fond of boasting the Mallandaines were a fighting race.

Why should he resign romance, innocent love, an embodied poem ? Why fling aside a flower, even it had been thrown in his path and fallen at his feet, among the gaudy peonies of the vice-trodden stones of Regent Street ?

Should he let Nellie fall more utterly in love and amuse him, as if she were some new but lovely specimen of original young female ?

But no ; this was not his way.

He was not selfish, but terribly tired and hopelessly depressed.

It would not be so very difficult to fall idiotically in love with Nellie for herself, but the heir to ten thousand a-year proposing to a girl who had never heard of 'Butters' Spelling Book,' or the History of England, of five-fingered exercises for the piano, would be about as insane an act as that of the duke who married an American oyster-girl.

'The best way will be never to see her again,' thought Leonard.

But what is this languorous charm stealing over his senses, dispersing *ennui* and care ? Nellie's little speeches had indirectly cheered him, the innocent revelations of her thoughts, her wild enthusiasm and latent poetic despair, forced itself on a mind rich in that ideal faculty which, if it makes not a painter or a poet in creation, at least does so in appreciation.

'Whatever will become of her ?' he mused. 'She'll never stay with the Foggs, but be perpetually running away after me, like a dog that nobody wants, and that will not bear a chain, and what on earth am I to do with a girl who says she's willing to die for me, and thinks it all perfectly right and natural ?'

Captain Mallandaine thought of breakfast for the first time.

He rang the bell, ordered fresh relays of strong black coffee, glanced indifferently at the newspaper, seizing at last one of his strongest cigars, and, answering Vivian Branscombe's letter, tried to forget the memory of Nellie Raymond, the soft pressure of her lips, and the witchery of the sweetest voice and eyes in the world.

'Poor old Vi,' he muttered. 'Wants me to join them in the yacht, and talk about art and poetry, which she religiously hates, as the great green waves roll by, and the moonlight throws up her pearl-like complexion. No, my dear Vivian, I am too susceptible to the marvellous utterances of the ocean. Your worldliness would clash—you pretty mixture of dynamite and clay—and I should be thinking of my poor little dunce Nellie here, who is like one of dear old Burns' poems—a jewel in a rough setting, but, oh, how precious to the heart.'

When Nellie returned to the cottage, the gardener rushed out into the passage, caught her by the shoulder, and dragged her into the room, his face white with rage. Black-legged and terrible, he resembled one of those caricatures of Don Quixote attacking a windmill, so dear to the popular intelligence.

Mrs Faculty was wringing her hands and crying.

'Little devil,' said Faculty, using strong language. 'Little monster,' spinning Nellie round and round like a top, 'what have you to say for yourself? To come here and eat and drink with us, and then to destroy our property—'

'Three pounds gone—literally wasted,' sobbed Mrs Faculty, who was a saving woman, and slept with a stocking full of sovereigns under her pillow every night. 'Might as well 'ave pitched it into the gutter, and me a tryin' to draw the seams together—a pretty thing, indeed, to cut the master's best coat to pieces.'

'And then to see her flyin' through the park on Rosicrucian—why, he won the Dartmore Stakes last week—and our Captain looking as cross and glum as could be. She shall go to a reformatory.'

Faculty's strong hands were very painful. Nellie shuddered—she had before heard of a reformatory, and pushed the golden masses of hair off her forehead with a cry.

Her little ears were scarlet.

Faculty had pulled them deliberately between his sentences, as if they were aggressive commas, bidding him pause, and Nellie was shut up in her room for the rest of the day.

The next morning a loud double knock resounded on the modest green-painted door, and a splendid curricle and pair was being driven away towards the Hall stables.

Mrs Fogg had opened the outer door, and was welcoming their eccentric lodger with all the effusion that a woman who had read 'Pilgrim's Progress' twice through during her sixty-five years could manage to express.

'It's well, indeed, sir, you've come,' said Fogg, going out into the passage, and altering his former bass tones for the more flute-like and metallic whine that made women weep in chapel, and even startled refractory infants into silence.

'Ah, welcome as the flowers in May!' said the future Marquis de Rocheville, who had not yet heard the sequence.

He looked like a glittering basilisk, accustomed to courts from boyhood.

M. Lepelletier was now dressed with the perfect *chic* of a modern French dandy.

He was a true Parisian, a member of the Jockey Club, and since he had come into a fortune he generally backed all the wrong horses with an enthusiasm incredible in a man who hardly ever won ; he had the nose of a bird of prey, and dark, swarthy skin ; he was slightly rouged, and his moustache had been so constantly gummed and oiled by various brilliantines and cosmetics that it now darted out all over his mouth like the prongs of a thin garden rake ; he wore a black tie and blue frock coat, his boots were new, and he was what the French themselves would call '*très beau garçon.*'

This agreeable individual, in developing his dandyism, had endeavoured to forget his *grande passion* for Aurelia Mallandaine, but he had resolved on insisting that Leonard should grant him an interview with the unhappy victim of his cousin's treachery. In indulging his natural taste for dress, he forgot heroics, and wished simply to appear as a gentleman of the first rank and fashion combined. If Aurelia were sufficiently sane, she might then appreciate the mistake she had made in having preferred the cavalry officer, De Beriot, to himself. It was not a very delicate way of looking at the matter, but a man who has been severely snubbed and fifth-rate for years, naturally remembers, and the free use of absinthe and liqueurs, and cigars had dulled the not too keen sensibility of the *beau garçon.*

Fogg's eyes took in this extraordinary picture at a second glance; the gardener had never seen so marvellous a metamorphosis. Where had vanished the slouch hat, the thick dogskin gloves, the long hair and blackened pipe ? He understood M. Lepelletier was rich, but the arrival of the curricle and pair, and of himself so transformed, startled Fogg out of his usual passivity. The Frenchman was more cynical than ever, but this time he dazzled—and he was beloved

by a woman whose genius should have enchanted the world.

Some knowledge of Laura Branscombe's
enslavement may have given fresh light to
his eyes, jaundiced as they so often were ;
some sense of her extravagant worship may
have banished that moral spleen which
poisoned his life.

'This young girl you brought to us as
helper, sir,' said the gardener, morosely, ' does
no end of harm.'

He looked delighted, and his expres-
sive eyes flashed warm admiration on
Nellie ; that blonde loveliness was finer
than the ordinary pink-and-white prettiness
of others.

'Wants teaching, eh, Faculty ?' he said,
airily taking out a silver cigar-case, inlaid
with fine tortoise-shell, ' and breaking in, and
that sort of thing ?  What a complexion the
girl's got—superb !'

'Wants locking up, sir, in a reformatory,
and a good whipping.  Just look how she's
cut my best coat to pieces.'

'Oh Nellie, Nellie,' said M. Lepelletier, laughing, ' is this the way you mean to
renounce the world, the flesh, and the devil ?
Well, Fogg, don't look sulky.  What's the
damage ?  Will five pounds square it ?
And now tell me in what hath thy ser-

vant sinned ? Sit down, Nellie, and don't cry. I'll take care of you—always meant to, *parole d'honneur.* Dry your tears with your pocket-handkerchief, and be happy.'

Alas! she does not possess that necessary article. Her cotton sleeve goes to her poor little eyes again.

M. Lepelletier good-naturedly throws her his own superb cambric one, delicately scented, and possessing a large coat-of-arms, resembling a small Stilton cheese turned upside down, with a Latin motto in one corner, the whole worked by Laura Branscombe's own fair hands.

Nellie dives after this splendid work of art, and seems afraid to touch it ; she then sits down demurely, thankful that he seemed inclined to befriend her.

' When we came down yesterday morning, sir, expecting our breakfast, and a fire lighted, who should we see but that saucy minx walking with but Captain Leonard.'

' So soon ? ' said Lepelletier, shrugging his shoulders. ' Timon clearly improves.'

Fogg had never heard of that misanthropic heathen. He continued effectively,—

' I went after her, sir, directly, just as I'd knock a wasp off a pear, and when she came in I reproved her sharply, and gave her notice, telling her I would find her employ-

ment away from here—I hope, sir, I know
my duty—when she runs upstairs and cuts
my coat-lining, and, hang me! dances off
again after the Captain, persuades him to
show her the horses, and then tears away
on one like a jockey three times round the
park.'

'Nellie, is this true?' said M. Lepelletier, looking still more delighted—indeed,
quite loving.

'Yes, sir.'

Nellie here hung her head.

'Cheer up, little girl.   I've an idea.'

She refused to cheer up, and again burst
out crying.

'How would you like to go to school and
be taught beautiful things like a young lady,
eh, Nell?   Go in for the light genteel,
and all that—beginning with A B C and
ending with champagne suppers.'

He was very glad to find this 'last 'moral
gun' had missed fire as far as Fogg was
concerned.

'I should like it above everything,' said
Nellie, thinking of her idol, and longing to
surprise him with her cleverness.

'Well, then, being rich, I can afford
to be generous.   I'll pay for your education.   Give her a glass, madame, of
your best cowslip wine,' addressing Mrs

Fogg, whose apple-green eyes had again sought the cobweb, 'and look upon Nellie as my little *protégée*. Perhaps we'll make her a singer, or a dancer, or—heaven knows what ! '

Fogg here appeared to be praying silently, horrified at the Frenchman's levity. Mrs Fogg tried to look sympathetic as she picked up the five pounds and nimbly conveyed them to a long brown silk purse, from which they would ultimately rest in her grandfather's stocking.

' Tell the old boy you're sorry, child,' whispered M. Lepelletier, going up to Nellie and offering her a rose from his coat.

' No, that I won't,' flushing scarlet, ' now you've paid him. He's a horrid old wretch, and I hate him.'

'*Impayable !*' cried the Frenchman. 'She's delicious—*l'audace, toujours l'audace.* I'll make her the fashion by-and-by.'

Nellie was afraid lest those thin dark spikes surrounding his mouth meant to descend on her head. Mrs Fogg had hospitably brought out long-necked wine glasses, ' seedy cake,' and cowslip wine in a cut-glass decanter, all of which the future marquis declined with the air of a prince. He had lunched sumptuously at the ' Woman in

White'—the one hotel in Brooksmere—off hashed duck and beans an hour ago, washed down with Moselle.

He hated Leonard for keeping his sister here in secret, although he was particularly grateful to him for killing de Beriot.   And he meant to see Aurelia again.   He wanted to study the ravages time and anguish had effected in her supreme loveliness.

He was as subtle in his intelligence and feeling as Rousseau, and there was morbid satisfaction in beholding the wreck of the glowing beauty who had dared to despise him.

Mesmerism had revealed the hopeless misery of the woman he had loved so madly, and now he had come resolved on an interview.   He must behold the sweet brow and eyes, with their terrible stamp of grief. He must carry away the memory of a word, or tone, or gesture with which to soothe his imagination when absent from her.

Her mind had given way, but she was not utterly mad.   She would remember him, and he fancied that, attired as a man of fashion, some faint resemblance might be traced in his features to those of his cousin Oscar de Beriot.

At that moment quick steps were heard outside on the narrow path.

Nellie knew whose they were, and coloured, and spilt her cowslip wine over her apron with an involuntary tremor of the hand. It was Captain Mallandaine.

Lepelletier went out rapidly to meet him, but the two men did not shake hands.

'Who am I like?' said Lepelletier, in a dull whisper. 'Ah, you know, Leonard. Do I not resemble the man whom you slew in your just rage one grey morning amid the Flemish fields? You are alone answerable for his death. Am I not like him—your enemy — Aurelia's lover — Oscar de Beriot?'

A bitter smile curled about the Captain's lips.

'I see you know all,' he said coolly, '*Après?*'

'I have come, Leonard, to see her—your sister—the woman I still adore, the woman you have shut away in there,' pointing to the old Hall, 'and I insist on an interview.'

'I know you never spare,' said Leonard slowly, kicking a pebble from the path.

The hour he had so long dreaded had at last come. He breathed heavily, and leant against the clinging ivy encircling the cottage walls.

'And the day Aurelia sees you she will die,' he murmured, and turned away.

# CHAPTER X.

## THE ACCOMPLICE IN A CRIME.

 DRUNKEN actor, who in his time has played *Hamlet* to crowded audiences years ago, when actors were by no means so refined as now, in descending to play the miserable part of model to various careless painters, who regard him with the same indifference they might bestow on a cat or a parrot to be limned by them, naturally looks about for some more agreeable way of increasing a strictly limited income.

Bob Sidewing strongly objected to the mild nagging bestowed on him by his landlady, Mrs Maloney, when his modest earnings had been expended in whisky instead of in defraying the expenses incurred by the use of an attic on the fifth floor—a wretched little room, in which poor Bob took his meals and counted the woodlice climbing on the decomposed paper pattern, and smoked strong tobacco, as he cursed his fate and the evil day on which he made Martha Jane Appleby an ' honest woman.'

'That creature's been the ruin of me,' Bob would say, sitting on the edge of his little iron bedstead, while Mrs Maloney cooked his penny bloater. ' I know she's a bad 'un. I feel sure she'd stick at little short of murdering me if I nose again about Exeter and rake up the past ; but to Exeter I'll go, nevertheless, as soon as ever Mr Brook's finished his study of me as *Sir Peter Teazle.* Lord ! how sick I am of painters and painting, and the cramp and backache.'

Bob had one solace besides his pipe, and it was an ancient violin. Wonderful strains of music would float amid the attics—pastoral melodies, bringing before the tired sufferer's memory visions of clovered fields, green garden lawns, and pale lilac clusters. Without his pipe and his violin Bob must have surely paid a visit long ago to old Father Thames, and gone to sleep amid the slime and mud.

His music spread its charm even over the stuffy first-floor apartments, and Mrs Maloney would invite Bob occasionally downstairs into her kitchen, to be regaled on dried haddock and hot sprats, when she had visitors who could appreciate Shakesperian recitations and the melodies he would draw out of the beloved instrument, which he had picked up a bargain—in Wardour Street.

But something besides music and whisky, penny bloaters and studies of ' old men,' had now occurred to Bob. He had remarked that whenever any allusion was made to a little daughter supposed to have died and been buried while Bob visited the United States, his wife shuffled his questions and evaded his replies as if she feared detection. Detection in what? The daughter, to be sure, had been born before Bob bestowed his name on Martha Jane! but she had always been passionately fond of the child— almost, one might say, insanely fond of it— and he never forgot the surprise his wife manifested when, after an absence of six years from England, he had suddenly ap- peared before her, and was decidedly re- ceived with the ' cold shoulder ' women invariably offer to men they have learned to hate.

' I tell you, Bob,' Martha Jane had said, in deep contralto tones, strongly resembling those of a certain Mrs Macgregor who had played *Lady Macbeth* in Connecticut, ' that I'm sorry to see you. You've blighted my life and broken my heart. I wish I'd never worn your wedding-ring. I wish you were dead! The wild love I gave you years ago has grown into hatred.'

To do him justice, Bob believed his wife was half-demented. He never tried to soften her hatred, to win back her tenderness. She had frightened him with her murderous look and low-breathed words of vengeance.

And now he fancied he had this implacable woman in his power—that the snake was tame and trapped. Possessed with this delusion, Bob Sidewing had waited the due completion of 'Sir Peter Teazle,' and was now sitting in the small back parlour of that highly-respectable public-house, the Roebuck, with his old friend and crony of years gone by—William Diggory, the landlord, who had lived for the last five-and-twenty years in the 'Crooked Billet,' a stray corner of Brooksmere village.

Bob Sidewing had, like other men, done a good many foolish things in his time, but he had never successfully robbed anybody, or made money out of the misfortunes or weakness of others. The man who blunders, and robs his neighbours unsuccessfully, especially if he happen to be poor, is sent to prison, but Bob hadn't the capital or the chance given him to make a magnificent failure— ruin his butcher, tailor, and friends, and then

drive a beautiful carriage and pair ever after.
He had not the least intention of going to
prison or coming within the affectionate embraces of Jack Ketch.   He had both heard
and read of unfortunate men having their
heads jerked off under the maladjustment of
ropes and drops, and Bob's head was too
handsome and marketable an object to sell
to painters for their ' Sir Peter Teazles,' and
dying musicians, and old *bric-à-brac* men, for
him to run any risk of having it mangled or
otherwise maltreated.

But still, like the traditional roaring lion
seeking whom he may devour, the ex-actor
resolved to keep both his eyes and ears wide
open for any smart piece of business going
that might prove a gold mine to him.   He
had never robbed, but why should he not
levy blackmail on the rich ?   Family secrets,
like family diamonds, sold well.   Social
poachers of Bob's stamp could have a rather
good time of it, he knew, without being
under the painful necessity of sitting for
troublesome baronets and stupid old *bric-à-
brac* connoisseurs.

He had been a very ' merrie,' jolly soul
in the good old times when he enunciated,
' You should not have believed me.   .   .   .
I loved you not,' and brought roars of
applause from the gods in the gallery, while

his 'Alas, poor Yorick! I knew him well,' arrested the last succulent morsel of the juicy orange from gliding satisfactorily down the throat of some youthful chimney-sweep.

But now he was old—age must come—and his back ached cruelly from the various positions in which his natural tormentors, the painters, insisted in putting him for a shilling an hour. Bob had even been insane enough to try his hand at light fiction at a farthing a line; but his powerful, sensational story, although it had three double murders and suicides, was not too well received, and the 'Inspired Fiend; or, the Mystery of a Love Charm,' went ultimately to light Mrs Maloney's copper fire on a frosty morning in December.

Bob had, moreover, discovered that there was a certain 'loose screw,' a sort of revolving peg, which he thought in the future might be turned to good account, somewhere in that superb mansion of the Branscombes at Prince's Gate, with its three enormous drawing-rooms, all leading into one vast apartment through the withdrawal of slides and panels.

Like Israel's king, Bob had found there was little good under the sun, but that peg was worth driving at, and on to this loose screw, over which Martha Jane Sidewing, his better half, presided, would he attach himself, and extract therefrom those nice golden guineas, that promised better things than sprats and bloaters, cheap whisky and mouldy jam, from which Bob's artistic soul revolted.

'I made an honest woman of Martha Jane,' he would say in reference to that objectionable female. 'It's only fair she should try and keep an honest man of me, and times are so extremely bad, and Copenhagen Street is so extremely musty, that if Martha Jane don't wish that loose screw in the Prince's Gate household to tumble out, she must behave generously, or I shall be driven to harsh measures, and make more inquiries in a certain matter my beloved M. J. seems singularly anxious to avoid.'

Thinking of this, Bob had come to Exeter, and moved by a still more virtuous desire of investigation, he had journeyed to Brooksmere village, and was still seated on a large wooden chair behind a basket of white clay pipes, at the Roebuck, when the two men Percival and Musgrove entered.

There was also another man outside in the porch, bearing the appearance of a tramp or gipsy, in a dirty, loose white jacket, fustian trousers a good deal the worse for wear, and a billycock hat, who took stock of Bob's

handsome head and profile through the
parlour windows above, especially when that
head was bent over some golden coins, which
Bob imprudently filtered through his fingers,
to startle Diggory the landlord.

Bob had scarcely perceived the man.  He
only thought of Mrs Sidewing's donation of
ten pounds, and how very useful and pleasant
money was at all times and seasons.  He
did not recollect Martha Jane's laugh, nor her
words of rage as she clenched her hand and
cursed his ascending form up the area steps.

A passionate woman, this ill-used wife of
his, he admitted, though plain and pock-
marked—with a decided touch of the diabolical.

Bob regarded the two new arrivals with
but languid interest.

To descend to the varied excitement and
amusement of a rat-fight in the back premises
of the Roebuck might suit these men, but
hardly an actor, for rats were brisk, lively
little brutes, he knew, with a knack of flying
at a man's throat when too hard driven.
Bob was in truth no sportsman.  He handled
a gun like a true Cockney, keeping his eyes
on the barrel as if it meant to explode.

'What d'ye think o' that cider, Bob?'
asked Diggory, as he was drawing some prime
bitter six for the other two men.

'Well, I can't say, my friend, that cider's much in favour with me, for when one's teeth are shaky, and the best of 'em can be taken in and out, why, cider's bad stuff to swallow,' said Bob, with the air of a man who has a wine-cellar at home of rarest vintages. 'Come, I'll pay for a bottle; so square up, and let's have a drink before the battle.'

Bob paid for the ordered bottle of the best '47 out of his wife's recent donation; and as he spun the sovereign in the air, he paused, and recollected Martha Jane's wiry form and little weazel-like eyes, with their fiery glow, as if the whirlwind of passion had so convulsed speech that nothing was left for the utterance of thought but gesture and expression.

How long could he calculate on fresh donations?

The tramp outside, who had drawn some water in a cup out of Diggory's pump in the yard, looked in again at the parlour.

'Do any of you fellows know anything about the Branscombes of Prince's Gate?' asked Bob, indifferently, after each had drained his second glass.

'Branscombe?' echoed Percival. 'Why, ain't that the name of the people our Cap'n visits in the season?'

'Ay,' said Bob, replenishing their glasses;

'that's it. Try a smoke, you chaps. The
rats and dogs can rest a bit, and won't eat
their heads off by waiting.'

He handed round a pouch full of strong
tobacco, inwardly blessing Martha Jane and
her money.

The tramp outside laughed. He had got
hold of the tough end of a stale mutton chop
given to him by some well-meaning cook in
the village, and his laugh was not pleasant.

'Ah, Bob, you're so generous with your
money when you've got any,' said Diggory,
pocketing six shillings for the wine, 'that
your friends must look after you that you
don't come on the parish.'

'Friends!' echoed Bob, lifting his glass.
'My only friends are my guineas.'

'Didn't some one move outside?' asked
Bob, opening the window and looking out.

The tramp remembered his trade.

'For pity's sake, sir, a little bread or a
stray copper, just to 'elp a poor man on 'is
way. Six starving hinfants, gents all, an'
sick wife.'

Bob flung him a shilling.

The tramp thanked him, calling on all the
blessed saints to protect and save him, shoul-
dered his basket, and then sat down on a
little rustic seat near a gnarled oak in that
charming portion of Diggory's grounds set

apart for pleasure, and called, ' Tea-gardens ;
bowling-green ; hot water always ready,' and
where young couples watched the moon rise
above the mountains and feathery firs, with
their arms entwined, and congenial senti-
ments were interchanged, often ending in
' hot water ' and a breach of promise case.

' Didn't old Bernard Branscombe's first
wife leave him, and elope with an Austrian
wine merchant ? ' asked Bob, who knew
every particular.

' So they say.  I wish to heaven mine
would ! ' said Percival, who, after a third
glass was apt to enunciate strong anti-matri-
monial views.

' Well, heaven be praised ! ' said Bob,
theatrically, taking out another sovereign,
and spinning it round on the table, ' I've as
good a wife as ever man was blessed with
here below.   To be sure, she's not what
you might call much to look at.'

' Wot's looks ? ' cried the other two men.

Diggory said nothing.   He was addicted
to sultanic weaknesses, the neighbours said.
No one had ever seen a Mrs Diggory, but
the landlord of the Roebuck admitted that he
had been disappointed in love, and was not a
' marrying man.'

' A man wants a tidy wench as 'ull scrub
is floors, and cook a decent dinner, and put

by money for a rainy day, but a woman with
a dozen kids at her heels, a-screamin' and
a-yellin', and never one of 'em taken off, and
not a quiet corner for a man to 'ave 'is glass
or smoke a pipe in after 'is work, why, better
be a single man like Diggory 'ere.'

Still Diggory never spoke. This rural
Lothario thought of his Calistas with a smile,
although he ought to have looked guilty.

'Oh, but looks count, my friends,' said
Bob wickedly. ' Don't you like the feel of
your arm round a pretty waist, and a pair
of red lips pressed against yours, and the
glance of a merry eye ? '

Diggory nodded slyly. He quite understood Bob, only he was too prudent to
avow it.

'Without love,' said the actor, with suppressed emphasis—'oh, believe me, without
love this world of ours is but a wintry plain
—a summer without birds and flowers—a
garden of weeds at the best.'

'But the worst o' pretty ones is they're
only fit to look at,' said Musgrove, who had
married a plain party, a greengrocer's widow,
with savings in the county bank. ' There's
that young lady's likeness hanging in Cap'n's
study—as pretty a gal—and, mind, I know
wot the quality ought to be—as ever you set
eyes on ; but I wouldn't trust that there

young woman with the life of a kitten—if I loved it.'

'Wouldn't ye, now?' said Diggory, on neutral ground at last. 'That's very curious.'

'What's her name?' inquired Bob, indifferently.

'Miss Vivian Branscombe. I saw it written under the portrait when I came for orders about the 'unters goin' down to Exmoor.'

'Vivian Branscombe!' echoed Bob, and smiled to himself as he took stock of his own likeness in the glass. 'Engaged, is she? And mighty fond of the Captain, I suppose?'

'Ah, but she's not got 'im yet. He's a rum 'un, is master; not like hofficers mostly are, but they do say he fights like a lion, and as for pistol and sword exercise, he's quite A1.'

'Is Miss Vivian Branscombe engaged to your master?' again asked Bob. And in spite of himself there came an odd tremor in his trained voice which Diggory alone perceived.

'That I dunno; but it's supposed, when we was in town for the season, they were engaged; for Cap'n, he dined there pretty well every night, and took her to the opera, and theayters, and concerts. I should say,' said Musgrove, taking a fresh pipe, 'he loved 'er; but all that's no sign, d'ye see, to go by, after all—quite the contrary; for real lovers play 'ide-and-seek with each other, and go white and red for nothing, and pass each other with their 'eads up, an' a-lookin' away, while all the time they're longing to jump into each other's arms.'

'Did you ever hear of a Nellie Raymond in these parts?' said Bob, after a pause.

'Nellie Raymond? Why, that's the name of the pretty gal in Faculty Fogg's cottage.'

Bob had retired into the regions of his mental arithmetic, but he had gained a point. The revolving peg was again threatened.

'Well, you fellows, ain't you a-goin' to bring out the rats, and let's 'ave a bit of sport?' asked the coachman.

Bob shuddered. It was a question of rats, not pegs, this time. He drew a piece of strong twine out of his pocket, tying his shabby trousers tightly round the ankles. The rats should not devour his calves, at any rate.

'Sidewing don't like the job, that's clear,' said Diggory, laughing. 'Why, if he hasn't gone and tied his legs in. Can't ye give us a bit of *Hamlet* in that costume, Bob?'

But the sight of the dogs, and the aspect

of a dozen or so large rats in a cage, to be let loose in a deep pit, were more than sufficient for the actor.

'Keep back the little dawg,' cried the tramp, who had ventured to join the party.

'Don't like that fellow's looks at all,' said Diggory; 'a regular cut-throat sort of a chap he seems.    I'll drive him off my premises.'

'Murder seems in the air to-day,' said Bob carelessly, pointing to the dogs.

As Diggory drove the tramp roughly off, he looked back once at Bob in a way that that must have considerably puzzled that philosophic soul had he seen him.

'How am I to do it, now, and earn the gold?' muttered the tramp, throwing his stick after a white rabbit scudding across his path.    ''Taint so easy to stick to a man like a pig, an' get off, but if he comes this way when it's dark, an' he's a bit easy in liquor, why, then—'

Murder was truly in the air.    How often men speak the truth in jest, and blunder blindfold to their fate!

A bolt was now drawn back from the cage, and the rats darted into the pit, the last one, however, bolting into a drain, from which he defied his persecutors, and blinded the plucky little terrier.

But Percival, suddenly pushing Bob aside, drew on his gloves, and kneeling down, put his arm and hand into the drain, and with practised coolness, dragged out the rat by his tail, but the little wretch, nothing daunted, flew at his enemy, and biting him clean through the finger, still hung on like grim death.

'Call that sport?' cried Bob, who was often chicken-hearted on occasions, beating a rapid retreat into the back parlour. 'All I can say is, it's sickening. I'd rather be excused from one of the little devils flying at my throat.'

The rat darted up a shed. Musgrove hit at it and it fell stunned, and was polished off by one of the dogs.

The dead rats were thrown from the pit, and the men thought of returning home, the terrier limping and whining piteously from a wound in his foot.

'It's a disgusting sight,' said the benevolent Bob from the porch, 'and I hope never to witness such another. What do you say to another bottle?'

Bob wanted to hear more of Nellie Raymond, but he did not wish his hearers to be aware of this; his profession as actor was in his favour; he could disguise emotion by manufactured light-heartedness, while his heart beat with anxiety. The bottle was brought and paid for, Diggory himself taking his fair share of the wine this time. The ''47' vintage seemed to overcome Percival, for, after a few vain attempts at speech, his head fell back, and as Musgrove threw a cloth over his face, he began to snore like a trooper.

But at that moment Bob gave a great start. He had never seen any face or form so fair as the one before him. Yes, long ago he remembered to have seen her equal —so very long ago—nearly eighteen years! Warm admiration kindled in his eyes.

Who was this girl in a straw hat and cotton frock, with some wild poppies and cornflowers, blue and tender as her eyes, fastened on the side with careless grace.

Bob had seen a great many young women going cheap at a shilling an hour as models, but never one to equal this; and why were the curling lashes black instead of being dead-gold coloured like her hair? and the eyes, were they darkest blue or violet?

'If you please,' said the voice, clear and flutelike, and that sent cold shivers down Bob's spine to listen to, 'can you tell me the best way to get back to Mr Faculty Fogg's cottage? I'm so sorry to trouble you, but I've lost my way.'

Bob knew her now.  This was Nellie Raymond, the girl he had been so long seeking,
the instrument through which he had
meant to make a fortune.  Martha Jane
had told him their little child was dead, but
Bob fancied after all she might have been
forsaken in some mad fit of rage by her
mother, and that he might find her again.

But all this was mere surmise, after all ;
he must go on safer ground.  Safer ground !
Alas, poor Bob ! when the tramp, by the
common's side, will wait patiently hour after
hour for his prey, and turn his knife in the
moonlight, and think of the golden sovereigns
he means to steal from a dead man's body—
the plenteous golden sovereigns promised to
him by a wicked woman if Bob is slain.

' Lost your way, have you ? ' said Bob,
puffing away slowly at his pipe ; ' but you're
not far out.  You must go straight across
Wincherly Common, pass the four cross-
roads, and that will bring you close to
Staplefield Hall.'

' Why, bless me,' cried Percival, waking
himself by a too musical snore, ' if that isn't
the young child that rode Rosicrucian !  How
came you here ? '

' Because I'm going to be a lady,' said
Nellie, with a smile.

' An' d'ye think a lady's a ready-made

piece o' goods? It takes years and years to be a lady, and a father and mother to name 'er, and lots o' schooling, and sweet ways, and money, and never say wot you raly mean, an' never 'ave wot you raly want,' sneered Percival, who was a true Conservative, and stood up for the interest of the landed gentry.

'Perhaps, then, if I was a servant I should do better,' said Nellie mischievously, with a wilful pout.

'Shouldn't wonder at all if ye stood out for a good price, and tossed yer 'ead,' said Musgrove sarcastically. ''Tisn't all the full bags that stand up stiff and straight as men like, and a lady's a pore creature when times are bad, and there's something else wanted besides screamin' at a pianner, and novel-reading, and shopping.'

'A lady?' echoed Bob. 'Well, I should say you were one of nature's ladies, my dear, and don't want much making.'

'It's nature that 'as to be driven out of a lady,' said Percival, laughing.

'Oh, but it will be so lovely to be taught,' said Nellie, 'and I'm going to school, and shall never be very much scolded any more.'

'Why, when were you scolded?' asked Bob, who saw an opening that might lead to the information he wanted.

' At the circus, when I was tired.'

' Circus !' echoed both the other men ; ' but, there, we might ha' known it. Only a natural born jock could a-ridden our thoroughbred without a bridle.'

' What circus, my dear ?' asked the watchful Bob. ' Don't be shy ; we'll do ye no harm. Come and sit down by me, and rest before your nice long walk over Wincherly Common.'

' I never liked the circus,' said Nellie, innocently, evading his question, ' and that's why I ran away.'

' And who were your father and mother, my dear ? 'Tis a wicked thing to let a pretty lass like you be exposed to the temptations of cities, which are ravenous and destroying as wolves.'

Bob drained his glass of port, and both looked and felt for once extremely virtuous. He was on the right track at last ; the loose screw could be safely threatened.

' I never had any regular parents like other girls,' said Nellie, sighing. ' I don't know anything about them. Madame Juanita Dalton made me call her " mamma " once, when she wanted some money out of a funny little gentleman she called Duke Tommy, and there was an old woman, with very small eyes and awfully pock-marked, who came to see me when I fell through the net and was laid up. She gave me stories about Mrs Potiphar and a coat of many colours, and said she'd come again, but she never did.'

Bob's teeth suddenly assailed his nether lip.

'You said little eyes and pock-marked. Perhaps she was your grannie, my dear.'

'And now I must run away,' said Nellie, 'for they'll wonder where I am. Of course you know I'm not going to work any more, but be a lady, and wear lovely silk dresses like you see in the beautiful shops in Regent Street.'

'Another Duke Tommy, I suppose?' said Percival laughing, 'or, rather, friend o' the family. Who's going to pay for 'em, I wonder?' winking desperately at Bob, who endeavoured to look shocked and failed.

Nellie did not hear them. She was busy arranging her hat at the glass. A sort of half-drunken desperation seemed to have seized Bob Sidewing as she glided from their sight.

'The likeness!' he muttered, 'the marvellous likeness! Oh, Martha Jane, you smiling serpent, you shall pay for this! Let me starve, will you, and tell me ten pounds is the last penny I'll ever get! Ten pounds!

Pah ! a thousand wouldn't make me hold my tongue now. I'll have an annuity out of you and Miss Vivian Branscombe, or I'll let in daylight and somebody else at the same time.'

# CHAPTER XI.

### THE FOOTPRINTS IN CUT-THROAT LANE.

LONG after Percival and Musgrove had left the Roebuck did Bob and Diggory prolong their sitting. They drank a great deal more than was prudent, but the landlord enjoyed Bob's society, which, in its way, was, when he liked, brilliant and refined; and Diggory found Bob a good listener, and many were the *bonnes histoires* the two men recounted till their tongues began to cleave ominously to the roofs of their mouths, while their lips became parched, and a fiery spark seemed to dart like a snake in their throats.

'A fine night,' said Diggory, opening the window, and watching the silver moonlight spread over mountain and woodland. 'No need to offer you a lantern this time, old friend, to find your way back to Brooksmere.'

Bob was astonished to find the difficulty he had to reach his hat and put it straight on his head.

Diggory had by this time lighted an oil lamp, and held it up over Bob, while Bob was possessed with the insane delusion of trying to light a twopenny cigar through a rushlight shade placed on a shelf in the landlord's table.

'Why not stay the night, Sidewing?' asked his friend. 'There's the blue room at your service.'

'No,' said Bob, 'I'm all right, fresh as a buttercup. I'll maybe look in to-morrow before I go to Exeter.'

He had now attacked a small mulberry tree with his knotted stick.

'I thought I was running against Farmer Oats' black wall,' said the actor, with sundry see-saw movements. 'Good-night, Diggory. Give us your hand.'

The hand was extended, and the two men parted with indistinct but kindly leave-takings.

Bob walked on very rapidly the first quarter of a mile past the corn fields and meadows, then he began to loiter about. He fancied the moonlight was too strong for him, for what made his eyesight all misty and queer? He mistook a large oak tree for a church, and thought he should like to go to sleep in the trunk with the squirrels.

' Lord ! how strong Diggory's wines are !' muttered Bob, throwing off his hat, and sitting down by the tree.

He was now, though he hardly knew it, on the borders of Wincherly Common, before gaining which he had to pass through a very lonely lane with wide-spreading bushes on each side, called by the villagers ' Cut-Throat-Lane.'

Down this cheerful pathway, with its deep ruts caused for years by heavy cart-wheels, Bob passed in the moonlight, with his knotted stick over his shoulder, and here he again turned dizzy, though not from the moonlight, for the overhanging bushes and trees in the lane were too thick to permit the entrance of any silvery rays of light.

' Could you just give a pore feller a six-pence ?' asked deep, hoarse tones at that moment, and the voice so startled poor Bob, who was a nervous man, and never very brave at the best of times, that he almost screamed.

' Come, you white-livered coward, tip up your gold, or I'll make this 'ere lane earn it's name to-night,' said the tramp, who understood the man he had to deal with. ' I'm in earnest. D'ye see this ?'

He had drawn out a horrible weapon from a basket, a double-bladed sailor's knife, and brandished it in the air.

This time Bob screamed aloud. The tramp rushed on him, and being a very strong and powerfully built fellow, held one hand over Robert's mouth, while with the other he tried—to use his own term—to ' knock him silly.'

Terror and agony, combined with the effects of the drink, were rapidly producing syncope. A blue, death-like look spread itself over the actor's face, his muscles twitched, he groaned and beseeched mercy in inarticulate accents.

He knew, in his weak, dizzy state, that to wrestle with the robber would be worse than useless, and those heavy thuds on the back of his head would, he believed, end by giving him paralysis or congestion of the brain.

' There, give over whining,' said the tramp, flinging Bob, half senseless, from him into the ditch, ' becos, I tell ye, you're a dead man. I've took an oath to kill you—I've sworn it. Night an' day 'ave I been a-waitin'—waitin' long.'

The steel blades of the knife now flashed with deadly significance before Bob, — he must make one last appeal, his senses were fast forsaking him, but he remembered his golden guineas wrung out of Martha Jane in the back kitchen at Prince's Gate.

'Take the gold,' said Bob, panting, and half suffocated from the oozy moisture of the ditch, 'and save my life. Five sovereigns—there, you can take 'em. I never harmed you—I never did you a wrong. I'm a poor old man, very old and weak, and half dead from your blows.'

There was no answer; but where Bob was lying a break in the thick bushes enabled him to see a reflection of the moonlight on the tramp's face, then he knew there was no hope, and that he must die.

The robber took the five sovereigns from the half dying man, and then some over-mastering fury found vent in words.

'Ah, you know me now,' said the tramp, 'and you know another five minutes will settle ye! I'm the man you 'ad took up for stealin' your fur coat five years ago. I went to prison. I've never found a friend since. I've been 'unted down like a mad dawg, an' I told ye, didn't I, as I'd do for ye one day—an' I waited. Work! As if I could find honest work with the brand of a gaol on me! Friends! As if the craven brutes 'ud put out a little finger to save me! Wife died o' want, and two little 'uns followed. D'ye know wot it is to be starving—driven from place to place with no character—no nothing? And I says to myself, " There's one to thank for this—the devil that sent me to gaol and killed my Kitty and her babes—him as dragged me down!" Ah, there's others as hate ye too, but not like me ; for mine is a burning fire night and day.' He wrenched a woollen jersey off his chest as if that raging fire must be slaked by human blood. ' So die—die—die!'

He held his knife high in the air above Bob, and brought it down on his body with fearful force—such force that the yellow, muddy water in the ditch turned to crimson, and with a dying groan the wretched man's head fell backwards on the bank.

' That's done for him at last,' said the tramp, drawing the blood-stained knife on the dewy grass. ' He'll never 'ave the chance to send another pore starvin' cove to quod—never. If that isn't justice, wot is ?'

He ran with all speed on to the main road, while Bob lay forsaken and alone in a ditch.

Presently a white form crept from the other side of the bushes, and a thin young man—one of Farmer Oats' carters—peeped through the prickly hedge, and saw Bob's handsome profile upturned in the moonlight.

He was called by the neighbours Timothy Hare, through his want of courage, but he had a good heart, and he could not leave that poor old man, with a face like St Thomas the Martyr, to perish in a wayside ditch.

'A drop o' brandy might revive 'im,' thought Hare. 'I wonder, though, if he's real dead.'

He lifted the actor in his arms—Bob was light and spare, and thin from scanty nutrition, work, and worry—and carried him tenderly across the meadows back to the Roebuck, where Diggory, mixing a final libation of hot shrub, was now sitting *tête-à-tête* with the baker, Mr Canary, an incorrigible night bird, and fond of a glass.

' Please, sir, he's been murdered,' said Hare, trembling from head to foot, and staggering under his burden.

Canary was a churchwarden, and had his eye on him.

' Murdered !' echoed Diggory, placing his hand on Bob's heart ; then, as they laid the actor on the couch, turning quickly to Hare, ' Go to the village and bring back Dr Morris. The heart still beats—faintly, it's true, but while it beats there's hope.'

# CHAPTER XII.

## THE LIVING SHADOW.

'Sleep, what hast thou to do with her—
The eyes that weep with the mouth that sings?'

NELLIE walked very slowly back to the cottage over Wincherly Common after her interview with Bob Sidewing. She was free at last. And why was she free? Through what magic process had she escaped the heavy penalties exacted from the poor? Every slave asks this. Why were her wishes to be unchecked—her hopes uncrushed—her nature no longer checked and cramped?

The answer was very simple. She had taken the fancy of a rich man whom Nellie believed possessed one of the best and kindest hearts in the world.

All her trouble had ended; she was going to school, and M. Lepelletier would pay for everything. How nice and comfortable it sounded! What a charmingly irresponsible state of affairs!

She might be a singer or a dancer, or any other agreeable fortunate nymph protected by a wealthy friend.

Yes, this was life at last; every one was going to be so good to her, and she could shower her affection on them in return, and never be hungry or beaten any more. It was like going to heaven—these rich, delicious thrills of joy, these bright sparkles of hope and pleasure on the rippling stream of fancies in a young girl's little ignorant soul. It began with rapture, and must end in triumph.

'How happy I am!' cried Nellie, half buried in the spreading fern, and gathering a great heap of wild flowers from under a damp hedgerow. 'I cannot, I never shall forget.'

It seemed to her, after that kiss from Leonard's lips, that she had entered a new world; the whole earth and air were filled with that marvellous electric charm the presence of a beloved one spreads on all around.

Who is it says the best of life is intoxication, and bids us drug our senses with ether, wine, or love? The confusion, the ecstasy, the fear were almost more than she could bear.

She was a fanatic in feeling and emotion from that hour. But this sweet revelation of another world, this consciousness of another's empire over her heart, completely changed the girl.

Deep crimson blushes trembled into life, new aspirations awoke; the woman's desire to hide henceforth all token or avowal of tenderness crushed out the girl's innocent little speeches, and made her resolve that by no smile, no touch, no whisper, would she let Captain Mallandaine know how she loved him.

And then she smiled and tore up her poppies and field flowers, and wished Leonard was looking just once more into her eyes— those deep, sombre, violet eyes, dark as the shadows on a waveless sea when the sky is reflected therein.

Poor Nellie was awaking to the tragedy of a woman's life at last; she wanted to hear more about love, and understand why she blushed and turned pale, as if she had a fever, and trembled for nothing. It was really very strange. It filled her with terror. And the strangest part of it all was that her tears were delightful; there was such sweetness in this new pain, it gave her the same sense of fulness and rapture as when she first learnt to pray, and knelt down and never questioned whether those in heaven heard her—the prayers sufficed.

When Nellie returned, the superb curricle and pair were drawn up just outside the lodge gates, and M. Lepelletier, in an equally superb fur-lined coat, was patting his horses' necks as if he had not yet grown tired of money's delights and power.

'Why, Nellie, where have you sprung from —been to sleep, or what, on the common?' he said, laughing. 'Your eyes look large and dreamy, as if kissed by the wandering breeze.'

'I've been thinking,' said Nellie, twisting her hat in her hand, and cracking the cheap straw, 'about your kindness in sending me to school.'

How pretty and happy this girl was in her young belief. He liked her child-like, unquestioning nature.

With Nellie he felt at ease, refreshed, and calmed. Laura Branscombe discomposed him. She was like some grand firmament in which are storms and thunder, troubled planets and restless stars; but Nellie was a flower, she never reasoned or questioned, she only grew, bloomed, and enchanted.

The tired man of the world, with his heartless codes and butterfly wooings, could not fathom the depths that are latent in all true

genius, but artless prettiness and fresh rosebud lips were a pleasant distraction.

'Lollie gets worrying,' he would say, rather
grimly; 'is jealous of my every thought.
We don't want to swallow a firebrand in a
love potion—*pardi*—but a pleasant, cooling
drink.'

'I've found you a school, Nell,' he went
on, rolling a cigarette, and flipping the large
buzzing flies off his steeds' noses. 'The
Misses Roby — Ruth and Rebecca — two
maiden ladies living at Myrtle Villa, Brooksmere Green. I'll drive you there in a few
days, and introduce you as my niece.'

'And suppose I run away?' said Nellie,
with a mischievous sparkle, cracking more
straws.

'Then, *ma chere*, you may go to the deuce.'

'Oh, sir, don't say that—I was only in
fun.'

'Little ingrate, listen to me; here is
your one and only chance of getting on in
the world. I don't think you'll ever pipe
louder than a canary bird, and you didn't
begin to study the graceful art of dancing
early enough, so what d'ye say, Nell, after
you're a little more learned, to being a dear,
pretty little milliner in Regent Street — a
charming improver—one of the 'young ladies'
who enjoy the privilege of a piano and well-

selected library when their labours are over for the day ?'

' Regent Street !' echoed Nellie, thinking of Leonard, and blushing furiously.

' But we'll see about that by-and-by.   Now, my little poppy-wreathed, rosy Phyllis, adieu for the present.   I shall get you some dresses and all that.   Fare thee well, Nell, my child ; give me that white rose growing by the wall, and now sheer off, for I'm going to drive the horses round.'

He threw aside his cigarette, buttoned his coat, caressed the thin spikes about his mouth, and, gathering up the reins, drove off with his air of prince and Samaritan combined, cursing his groom, however, in strong French, for not having been quicker in fetching a magnificent tiger-skin rug, with which he covered his well-preserved legs and patent-leather boots.

The Foggs were particularly amiable towards Nellie to-day ; she now excited a sort of reverential curiosity.   Faculty brought out some fine walnuts, and luscious yellow plums and peaches, gathering himself tempting red fruits from the orchard walls, while Mrs Fogg handed round the cowslip wine. And Nellie who was as fond of fruit as a gipsy or Asiatic, did complete justice to her dessert.

As she wandered after dinner through the

gardens and park in the drowsy autumn air, languor stole on her senses from the odour of the fragrant sweetness of the ripening fruits and crimson-hearted flowers. She abandoned herself to dreams as the autumn sun went down amid the corn-fields, and the distant whirr of a pheasant caught the ear.

We all know the peculiar effect of that sublime hush of the meadows, and how the country air feels about the temples as the crimson light tints the old woods and blue mountains with richer, ruddier glow. Exiles from England remember all this, and how the shady hawthorn looked in the spring when they saw it for the last time.

Nellie was so tired from her rambles that she went early to bed to-night, listening to the gardener's slow enunciation and measured explanations of various passages as he read a chapter from the Bible prior to bidding him good-night.

The moon had risen in a pale silvery mass as she undressed in the sweet odorous silence of the little room.

She liked going to bed by moonlight, watching the dim outline of the mountains, and hearing the rustle of falling leaves, and had just rested her head on the lavender-scented pillow, when she was quite certain there was a clear and distinct movement in the room.

She sat up in bed, her heart palpitating violently, as the moon was passing under a cloud, and something like a living shadow, or fugitive spectre, seemed to grow from out the wall.  All she had heard of haunted houses, ghosts, and, above all, the tales of the old tragedies enacted at Staplefield Hall, occurred to her mind.  But she was too terrified to scream.  Presently something rushed towards her, and a tall figure clothed in white, with loose hanging hair, clutched her, and with a smothered cry threw itself by her side.

Nellie's white breast heaved and fell like some lovely bird in the fowler's grasp, and then the eyes turned on her, the grip was loosened, and the woman spoke.

'Who are you?' she asked, in one of those rare voices in which one might almost say are tears.

'I am Nellie Raymond,' she said, shivering.

'I will tell you a story,' said Aurelia, looking curiously at Nellie, and moving one rounded arm in the air.

'There was once a fisher maiden, who always went out to fish in the early morning, and one day, as she threw her lines into the ocean, she drew out a ring.  This ring was really her genius, and it gained her at last a lover.  Tra-la-la!  But I am not going to sing,' said Aurelia, under her breath, the tears this time in her eyes as well as voice.

'She cannot be really mad,' thought Nellie sighing.

'They were to be married in the spring. She loved him so dearly; but one day, in the winter, she found a red rose growing in the garden. It was a sign her lover had been killed. Never gather red roses; let them grow,' said Aurelia, her thoughts straying again into cloud-land.

'After he was dead the fisher maiden always went and sat on the lonely rock by the sea-shore; but she never charmed any more lovers. She used always to see the red—the blood-red stain about his heart, the low-lying Flemish fields, and the dew and rain on his fallen head and hair—they were like the tears and kisses of her last farewell. And if she sang, there was no music in the tones; so she could only weep —weep—weep. People talk about death,' said Aurelia, the dreamy light in her eyes, and her voice growing passionate in spite of its pain, 'as if it were an end; but I know that he is sorry for all the anguish his cruelty brought me on earth, and that he longs to repair it. He is waiting to say, "Aurelia, dearest, gather the red roses; they will deck our bridal path—the beautiful flower-clusters, the purple passion-flowers blooming for us in Eden.'"'

Nellie laid her hand on that restless moving arm. She fancied that if Captain Leonard were to quite forget, or be killed, she, too, would abandon herself to similar grief—grief that fastened upon the mind, and slowly murdered it, like a venomous insect attacking a delicate fruit needing light and air and sun to foster its growth.

'I was always seeing the red roses,' said Aurelia, 'but I was not mad; it was only when I got tired of waiting, and the summer time tortured me, that I began to weep— when women weep much their brain goes— an incurable despair took possession of me; death was in my soul. Do you understand? Ah, no! you are too young and fair.'

'Yes, yes, I know,' said Nellie tenderly, turning to kiss her. 'Tell me more—it may comfort you.'

The pallid face looked still more bloodless after Nellie's embrace.

'The world seemed a huge wilderness after that red rose grew, but it will not be for long, for I am going home very fast; all my rings slip off my fingers, they're so thin.'

Nellie's nerves quivered. It seemed to her as if the evil fate that had triumphed over the wreck of this young life might also descend on her. Was this what love brought?

'I should have died long since,' she said in a hushed voice.

'Because you are weak. I was strong, that was the worst of it. Weak people give no trouble, but we who are strong, we linger for years; every part of us dies slowly and by degrees. They shut me up because they were afraid I should kill myself. I do sometimes want to hasten the end, but when I touch my fingers they get thinner, and my cough is worse, so I'm content to wait till the end. "Take care of her life," the doctors said. My life! Ah, they little know.'

Some impulse made Nellie lay her arms around Aurelia. She wanted her to believe how sorry she was, and Nellie, being a loving little soul, was now weeping in sympathy. She had slipped from the bed, and in her white night-dress, her hands clasped, looked like one of Lippo's golden-haired angels.

'Other women when they are like I am are shut away with strangers—that must be terrible, but I think Leonard, who killed my lover, never could have the heart to do that. If they shut my folly from the world, was not that sufficient? You are fair, but you are not like the woman he loved better than me, she who stole my ring.  She was beautiful and wicked, and had sapphire-like blue eyes—mine are dark and have lost their light.  She wore blue velvet and a collar of diamonds the first night I saw her at the theatre.  She was coarse, ignorant, and grovelling, but for all that she was a sorceress; all beautiful women are.  They brew poison in their cauldrons, and drug men to a deadly stupor that steals away their senses, aims, hopes, and ambitions, and destroys them body and soul, till both are shrivelled and lost.  She smote me unto death, though I pleaded with her.  Yes,' cried Aurelia, looking spectral again, 'though I humbled my pride to entreat her to see him no more, to leave me my lover.  But she only smiled at me in her cold, cruel way, and then turned aside, and kissed him again on the mouth, binding him closer in those crushing chains —and I shall be alone unto the end.'

'It is unjust,' burst out Nellie, still kneeling.  'Why are such things permitted?'

'There is no such thing as justice on the earth; it only lives and burns within our souls, and the craving for it consumes them. What was left to me?  Vanities, visiting, idling, hollow amusements, even art or ambition — how could I bear that false life of utter emptiness?  Better be the peasant woman with her babe in her arms, walking by her husband's side, than such a creature as I. But I never feel really mad till I see red roses, so when I die bury me deep in them, my hands crossed on my breast, holding masses of them, all heaped around.'

There was a movement on the stairs. Nellie heard Mrs Fogg's voice, and the sepulchral tones of her husband.

' They have come for me,' said Aurelia, shaking back her hair, and, opening the door, looked out and listened. ' Keep the ring,' she muttered, tossing one off her finger to Nellie, ' and now—farewell.'

She held out her wasted hand. Nellie seized it, pressing it reverently to her lips.

# CHAPTER XIII.

### DIGGORY'S ADVICE.

AFTER the doctor arrived, and Bob's wound had been dressed and all danger pronounced over, he sunk into that profound slumber which is considered a very favourable symptom of future restoration. The actor had escaped by one of those singular chances that occasionally happen to frustrate a murderer's fell design. He felt that after remaining a few days with his old friend Diggory it was his duty to return to town, with, however, the melancholy reflection that he was considerably poorer in pocket than when he started for Devonshire.

'I've had a blow, friend—a terrible blow,' murmured Bob, rolling his head, which still ached, from side to side on the chair railing, 'and what's more, there's foul treachery somewhere. There was a woman's hand at work in the business, I'm sure, and I firmly believe my wife prompted and designed the murder.'

' That's the worst o' wimmen,' said Diggory, lighting his pipe as the two men sat together in the porch, ' you never know what they're up to. Now, a man he'll mostly swear some good round oaths, or he ups and fights you, and you can protect yourself, but the wimmen are weak, and so they scheme. Yes,' cried Diggory, recollecting how one of his house-keepers had had him up for breach of pro-mise, ' they lie and scheme.'

' And now,' said Bob, thoughtfully, ' what shall I do ? I'm poor as a church-mouse.'

' You're getting an old man,' Diggory answered, re-filling his pipe ; ' you want to take it easy a bit. Will you follow my advice ? Checkmate your enemies by artful-ness. Let 'em believe you're dead, but all the time be up and doing—have your spies, and spy yourself, and to do this you must be disguised.'

' Ah, a good move. I'll be even with them,' said the actor. ' Mine is such a capital face to make up.'

Diggory had now plunged under the table, and was opening a drawer in a cupboard, from which he extracted a box covered with sawdust.

A very remarkable wig was now drawn

from under silver paper, one that the great Sheridan might have exulted over for one of his low comedy gentlemen.

'Try it on, Bob,' said Diggory, glorying in his idea ; 'and come before the glass to fix it.'

'What would Mr Brooke think of me now as *Sir Peter ?*' cried Bob. 'Why, it would delight his soul to paint me in this wig as an old Jew. He's long been trying to get such a curiosity. The public like to remember *Shylock*, for old Jews go off like snuff in pictures, as fast as they're painted. "Any shum you wantsh, sir, for good security, and only forty per shent,"' cried Bob, wheeling round in his wig, so that Diggory was convulsed with laughter.

'Stick to the wig, friend, if you want to be thoroughly disguised.'

'I'm dashed if Mrs Maloney would know me now,' said Bob, laughing ; 'or my bloodthirsty spouse, either. I'm going to make inquiries about our little girl who died when I was away in America, so she said, and I'll find out what became of her, and where she was buried. I believe Martha's been up to some bad tricks, and if I find there's been foul play, and that the child has been got rid of by underhand means, I'll land Martha Jane in Queer Street, as sure as my name is Robert Sidewing.'

His voice shook with suppressed rage, and in his new appearance of the Jew, he looked so much like *Shylock* bargaining for *Antonio's* flesh that Diggory again laughed heartily.

'A pair of false eyebrows will perfect you, and those you can get anywhere, and since we must part to-day—heaven only knows when to meet again—let's have a final glass for auld lang syne, while you put this thirty shillings in your pocket.'

Bob extended his thin hand gratefully.

'Heaven bless you, Diggory; you've been a good friend to me,' he said, huskily.

'And mind you write when that's gone for more if you're stumped. Alas! my *Shylock*,' cried Diggory, patting his shoulder; 'you remind me of my young days, when I was a merry spark, and Israel rejoiced over my bonds and parchments.'

'I feel very weak and wretched,' said Bob, stretching himself. 'Fancy leaving fresh linen, and all the sweetness and poetry of your hostelrie, grand scenery, yonder avenue of chestnuts, the still, hushed groves, and the music of fallen leaves and cascades, for my musty den in Copenhagen Street, earning a bare existence as a model. Isn't it hard, Diggory, what flesh and blood have to come to in this world?'

The good-hearted landlord had packed up

a large hamper full of provisions for Bob on his arrival at his lodgings, in which Devonshire mutton and Yorkshire hams collided, and Guinness's double stout rattled among biscuit tins and pots of cream.

After the wine had been quaffed, the good-bye said, and Bob, carpet-bag in hand, was again on the march, Diggory returned somewhat saddened to his hostelrie.

'A man of talent, that any one could see,' he muttered, watching Bob slowly disappear down the avenue of chestnuts, where he got smaller by degrees, and then wholly disappeared, 'lost through his own follies. Bob's one mistake always was, he never had enough conceit to push others out of his road, and it's your conceited ones that get the world to call 'em fine names and worship 'em. It's not what people's worth really is ; it's the vally they put on themselves, and the price they mean to get, and some prefer brass to gold—it makes more noise.'

Bob's reflections were interrupted by the sound of a loud railway whistle. He found he was very near the railway station, and soon overtook Diggory's boy, who had been sent on with the hamper. It was rather a singular coincidence that, as Mrs Sidewing was looking at the five sovereigns, all marked by herself, and handed to her by Dick as proof of her husband's death, Bob should be comfortably seated in a third-class carriage, *en route* for London, smoking strong tobacco and shaping his plans.

Meanwhile Nellie was being driven to Myrtle Villa, and when M. Lepelletier and his ' niece' descended from the curricle, the two Misses Roby, maiden ladies of the most indisputable respectability, both rushed to the window with the natural impetuosity of 'gushing young things' of five - and - fifty. How could they forget the polished grace with which the Frenchman had bowed over their ringless hands, and ever so gently squeezed their finger-tips.

' Look, sister,' cried Rebecca, bobbing her little head, adorned by its modest wisp of hay-coloured hair, over the blind, ' there he is again, and the girl with him.'

Miss Ruth Roby missed three stitches in her crochet antimacassar, and clasped her hands behind her back, a habit of hers when excited.

' Looks a sweet creature,' cried Miss Rebecca, greeting her new pupil with effusion in the drawing-room.

' Mesdames,' said M. Lepelletier, with a smile, ' here is the young girl, my niece, who will come to you after the holidays. With you I know she will be safe, both as regards her physical and moral welfare.'

The two sisters were making a graceful charge at Nellie in the form of cross-examination. Alas! she knew very little; had no idea of William the Conqueror, nor had ever heard of the Gunpowder Plot. But it was a comfort to think Nellie would not cry for three days, and refuse her dinner, and have to be shut up in the spare-room till she found her appetite.

'A most docile girl,' said the Frenchman. 'My dear dead sister, the Countess D'Arcy's only legacy to me.'

'How very touching!' murmured Miss Ruth, lifting her handkerchief to her faded eyes. 'A countess! Yes, she looks quite thoroughbred.'

M. Lepelletier here threw down a bundle of five-pound notes on the table.

'Help yourselves, ladies,' he said, with his gallant air, so different from that horrid Mr Stedman, the retired soapboiler, who doled out half-sovereigns when he paid his bill, and always took off five shillings and sixpence for his daughter Carrie's pew-rent.

The sisters modestly clawed three five-pound notes.

'Does that include everything, mesdames?'

'Yes, every extra.'

'You'll find my niece very ignorant, I fear,' gracefully apologetic. 'She was kept so constantly at her mother's side.'

'Precisely—so very natural,' came the answer, in the form of a duet.

Nellie looked from one to the other in unfeigned surprise.

'Ah, *ma belle,*' he whispered, resting his hand affectionately on her shoulder, as the sisters retired—one to fetch a receipt stamp, and the other to show him a coloured map, the work of Carrie Stedman, their cleverest pupil, 'you must be surprised at nothing. Who were your parents? How should I know, and what need you care? You interest me ; *petite blonde aux yeux bleux,* and when I'm interested—*pardieu*—I'm practical.'

M. Lepelletier yawned. He felt somewhat weary of benevolence and Nellie's society, so he made an excuse to get rid of her, and after leaving the villa drove off alone.

Nellie sauntered leisurely homewards, oppressed with a secret weight. Just as she swung back the large gates leading to the lodge, she saw Captain Mallandaine, his hat tilted over his eyes, sitting on the same rustic seat by the cottage window as on the morning after her arrival at Brooksmere ; he had often thought of her since that first kiss of love.

Nellie was very pale. She tried to avoid him and escape through the open cottage door, up the cork-screw staircase to her little room, but this he would not permit.

His thoughtful eyes fastened on hers, and then he nodded in a friendly way, very re-assuring to Nellie, and beckoned her to his side.

She looked so beautiful and wistful in her pale agitation, that Leonard's heart went out to her once more in spite of all his resolves.

Nellie abandoned herself to the bewildering fascination of the moment. This slow throbbing under a gaze was delightful, she could not speak, but looked grave and pensive.

'Come,' he said gently, 'and sit down here with me.'

Those dark, glittering eyes are again looking into her troubled ones. His hand is touching the sleeve of her dress ; the passion-flower waves above their heads. The little leaves fall one by one. The soft velvet lawns are bathed in sunlight, and they are alone.

'Nellie, have you no welcome for me to-day ? Not a word ?'

Nellie cannot speak. She thinks of Aurelia and the lost ring, the fisher maiden, and the red rose.

Who so timid as she who loves ? Silence is love's empire. He lives in dreams.

The place is hushed and calm, veiled with the rising of faint, white mists, and Nellie, with a complexion like the creamy fairness of a sun-warmed white flower, is lifting black silken lashes, on which tears tremble. She remembers that they must soon part.

'Where have you been all this time?' he asks.

She is certainly a dear little thing, and her wet eyes, dewy like large violets in the sunrise, look even more kissable than these quivering lips ; and yet he is trying to forget Nellie, and break himself of the delight of thinking of her.

'Wandering about. I'm going to school soon.'

'Indeed!'

'And I shall work so hard.'

'What—or rather, who—has changed your destiny?'

She notices now the least drawl in his tones. Nellie hesitates, and then she says abruptly,—

'Monsieur Lepelletier.'

'Our evil genius,' with a shrug.

'Isn't he a very kind gentleman?'

'Oh, very,' sarcastically ; then, *sotto voce*, 'The cursed spider! Why doesn't he stick to his wasps?'

Leonard tilts his hat this time straight over to his eyes, and sighs.

'Why do you dislike him?'

'Because I happen to know a thing or two

about him that are not exactly kind and Christian-like, to say the least.'

'Do you, *mon cher?*' said M. Lepelletier, who had driven round the other way, and hearing voices in Fogg's parlour, sat on the sofa by the window and quietly listened ; '*bien obligé.*'

'He's a duellist to begin with.'

'So are you,' Nellie answers hastily.

'Eh ?  Pon honour, you mistake.  I can defend myself—that is all, and if one is challenged, one can't refuse, can one—especially under certain circumstances ?  Lots of fellows —nice fellows, too—have cut Lepelletier.  I don't know why.  He wins heavily at cards sometimes ; but never mind him !  Tell me about yourself.'

How he enjoys watching her !  Passion goes through many processes in its development ; in its first stage looks suffice.'

'Ah, *mon cher,*' mutters the Frenchman, 'so you court the little rustic beauty, do you ? *Parole d'honneur ;* it's hardly fair—*perfide Albion !* and he's a soldier, too.   Deuce take him !'

'There's nothing to tell,' Nellie says shyly.

'Nothing ?'

'Well, very little.'

M. Lepelletier rises, chips some of the

dried grass in the vase into pieces, shakes himself, and caresses the thin spikes about his mouth.

Is he getting old ? Nonsense! *Vogue la galère.* Well, there's always Laura Branscombe and the best cosmetics.

'You little fairy, you've positively bewitched me,' says the captain.

And this time he has drawn Nellie to him, and an arm is around her waist, while a black moustache is pressed on the golden curls about her temples.

'Oh, don't, please, don't!' cried Nellie, with a little wild cry, struggling and trembling in his embrace.

'Why not?' asks Leonard exultingly, with a lover's thrill. 'Love me a little, Nellie, do! I'm so tired of everything, so miserable, don't you know, and all that. Be my dear little pet, won't you, child? and then, perhaps, some day—I must kiss you ; I can't help it, you little darling—some day all may change, and—'

'Hullo, Leonard! Where have you got to?' asks Lepelletier, coming round by the cabbages, and smoking a cigarette. 'Ah, *mon cher*, spoilt a *tête-à-tête*, I'm afraid!'

# CHAPTER XIV.

### THE NEW GROOM.

'And when she took a ride in the park,
Equestrian lord or pedestrian clerk
Was thrown into an amorous fever.'

'ACTUALLY refuses my invitation on board the yacht,' Vivian was saying, with a sickening heart, as she read the little trite note in which Captain Mallandaine, in acknowledging her charming portrait, yet declined to come within physical contact of its reflection. 'I wish I'd never written to him, or sent him my likeness. It never pays to run after men,' ended Vivian, ruefully, looking very pretty and girlish in her morning robe of light blue *toile d'Asie*,—a loosely-fitting morning robe that encased her slender body like a blue firmament, from which her throat rose like a fair pillar, or delicate white flower.

She renounced all idea of yachting since

Captain Mallandaine had declined her invitation. She was as much in love as a very fashionable court beauty, the leading *belle* of the season, nourished on vanities and admiration, can well be.

‘ And won't I snub him when he does deign to call,’ thought the beauty ; and something that stood in the place of ‘ soul ’ darted out of her eyes,—a spice of the devilry latent in every true daughter of Eve.

But the tears, after all, would come, and the throat twitched. Was she not positively forgetting to flirt scientifically ? What was this wretched kind of weariness and despair, producing the extremes of languor or vexation, and sapping the charms of everlasting amusement ?

Vivian had successfully resisted all other worries and discomforts till now, but the pangs of love were unconquerable in their violence. She loved the dark-haired soldier, with his strong codes of honour, his indifference, his gloom.

She gloried in the eager demonstrations he had received on his return from a tedious war, and had herself been present, wearing a rich violet *duchesse* satin, made a *à la Pompadour*, at a reception given in his honour, when all the tenants, young and old, on his father's estates, were regaled on the beef and beer so dear to every true-born Briton, followed by copious allowance of tea and plum-cake supplied to all the old women and children on the place, the entertainment winding up with a dance, in which Leonard waltzed with her in a carpeted barn, to the amazement and delight of the tenants, who had never seen a Pompadour costume. The music of the village yokels had made her shriek and shudder a little in good-natured horror. It was so very different, she whispered, from the Maelstrom band, or those of the Guards, or 10th Hussars.

She remembered the flags and triumphal arches, the speeches of various friends, the emotion of Leonard's father, his own simply-worded replies, and the tremendous volleys of cheering that had deafened her, while it enraptured.

All women glory in ovations to their heroes, and Vivian thrilled like some Greek or Roman maiden when the victor's crown is flung at the feet of the god of the hour.

' Can he have taken a fancy to some unpresentable neglected girl who doesn't know how to enter a room ?' mused Vivian, sitting before her white and gold mirror, dark lines under her eyes, and feverish spots on her unpowdered cheeks ; ' some blundering Phyllis out of a villa or cottage, whom he has caught in a pretty attitude at church? I believe heaps of fellows fall in love at first sight in church. Men are so idiotic. Given fair opportunities, lawn-tennis and a nice display of white muslin, pink cheeks, and a good head of hair, and it's all up with the simple-tons. Oh, Leonard—dear Leonard! I'm longing to torture you, pay you out, and make you miserable, and all the time some hateful village *belle* down in Devonshire, who can't ride or dress a bit, is perhaps winning your heart because you are tired and have nothing else to do.'

Vivian had never heard of the tragedy that had wrecked Aurelia Mallandaine's life. She was supposed to have died abroad among the nuns at the Convent of the Bleeding Heart.

'I suppose I'd better ride to-day?' said Vivian, speaking aloud.

She was very pale, and looked worn. The anguish of uncertainty, the dread of some danger about her path, were imperceptibly preying on her spirits.

Never since the loss of the diamond neck-lace, and the low-muttered words of Bob Sidewing, had Vivian Branscombe felt the same. She never alluded to the loss of that diamond necklace, but had one made exactly like it in the finest imitation paste possible, ordered in Paris of the most famous jewellers of the Palais Royal, so that none but a connoisseur or dealer in gems could have detected the difference, and somehow the sight of this hateful imitation necklace made Vivian turn hot and cold, and feel sick and broken, as if her life resembled it, and that it, too, was false and glittering—a mockery, like those paste diamonds in the old velvet case, all hollow and unsound beneath.

'You careless girl,' Bernard Branscombe had said lightly to her, as she told him the necklace had only been mislaid; 'didn't I tell you it would be found?  And you actually wanted poor old Martha Jane Side-wing taken up for the robbery.'

Vivian smiled, but said nothing.

Before ordering round her horse, King-fisher, this morning from the stables, Vivian paid a visit to her step-mother, Mrs Brans-combe, who was painting in her studio when Vivian entered.

Pale glimmers of golden light stole through the blinds, and Laura, in her black satin dressing-gown, trimmed with robings of rich ruby velvet, looked almost as fresh and brilliant as the likeness of herself, twenty years ago, that met the eye on entering, when there had been jewels in her hair and natural roses decked her corsage, and the blue-black tresses, escaping from a diamond aigrette, had fallen in ebon waves about the girlish bust and lily-white neck and arms— the portrait of Laura as *Juliet*, before her heart had withered as Bernard Branscombe's wife.

'Why, how pale you look, Vivian,' Mrs Branscombe said, going on with a background. 'Don't you sleep, or have you been dosing yourself with that dreadful chloral you seem so fond of?'

The studio was a magnificent room of sixty feet in length. Laura had designed and painted all the frescoes herself. It had a dark oak-stained floor, with costly Turkey rugs thrown down here and there; rare and valuable plants and exotics stood in every corner; large vases in Dresden and majolica were arranged on carved oak pedestals; Indian jars, of inestimable value—the presents of a Rajah who had fallen slightly in love with Mrs Branscombe on the occasion of his visit to Prince's Gate—ornamented the mantelpiece, which was composed of the finest tiles money could buy, and the goddess who reigned in this palatial room, with its tapestries, flowers, and pictures, might have sat for Cleopatra, Boadicea, Helen of Troy, or any of the grand, passionate women of old who were queens and adored by men.

It was a room adapting itself to those of

refined and artistic tastes. The clock itself was antique and a poem. The room was voluptuous, like its owner. Here the opium-eater might have sunk into soft slumber, ravished with sweet sounds and perfumes; the musician have dreamt of immortal harmonies; the artist interpreted his fairest rhapsodies; the singer intoxicated his senses with emotional enchantment—in this room was the only possible life for Laura Branscombe, whose strange duality of being made her differ from others. Here all the vivid intensity and passion of her soul rioted in colour, sentiment, expression, and form. She was too grand and cold for the trash of ordinary ballads and libretti. She had not the patience to perfect her gifts as a singer or a player, and be merely the passive exponent of others' ideas. No; she must create poems in colour or words—create beauty in form and expression, aided by the highest ideal art. Musical composition was beyond her, so she found small delight in music. In this room all the struggles of an emotional temperament found vent, and the pride and glory of her genius expended itself in painting. Fashionable gaieties, dinners, balls, *fêtes*, and dress were insufficient distractions for one who felt a pitying contempt for their votaries.

'Do I look pale?' said Vivian, glancing

towards the yellow streaks of light. 'Oh, it's because everything here is so brilliant and splendid.'

She almost envied her step-mother her gift. It might even bring forgetfulness.

'Miss Branscombe looks ill, nurse, I think,' said Laura gently, addressing Mrs Sidewing, who was peacefully knitting on the raised platform artists use for their models.

She might have been painted for one of those terrible old knitting women of Paris seated around the blood-stained guillotine, when the fairest land in all the world killed its children by thousands, and was laid waste by tyrants and assassins.

'Oh, there's nothing in the least the matter with me,' said Vivian, sinking gracefully back on a velvet couch.

It was the one terror of her life lest her repressed anxiety should be perceived.

'I've been painting nurse's head this morning,' said Laura, bringing out a large picture. 'It's such a remarkable face, I think. Poor dear old soul! she looks so haggard to-day. It is lined with suffering and the ravages of grief, isn't it, Vi? I'm painting her as a dying Niobe—worn and aged and ill; not the cool, blonde, well-preserved-looking young woman, with tears running down her face, one usually sees.

She must be old—Niobe wasted with anguish and weeping at seventy.'

Vivian shuddered a little at this likeness. She was really absurdly nervous to-day. It was painted with marvellous force and power. One seemed to fancy Niobe beating those thin hands restlessly together as she looked on at some long-contemplated revenge.

Mrs Sidewing looked less like a Niobe than a murderess, or a serpent thought Vivian, longing to mount Kingfisher and ride away her nasty fit of the blues.

'Why, my dear Vivian, you're positively trembling,' said Mrs Branscombe, who had some idea Captain Mallandaine's note had upset Vivian at breakfast—women in love are so keen over these things; 'and I declare, nurse,' feeling the girl's hand, 'she's quite feverish.'

'Lor', ma'am, what a fright you've made me!' cried Mrs Sidewing, who had never before seen any resemblance of herself.

'Fright!' echoed Mrs Branscombe enthusiastically—all true artists are enthusiasts. 'That's high art. It ought to make people cry to look at it. Can't you fancy how that hair slowly turned grey, how often the thin, parted lips must have quivered through those long seventy years? Yes, Vivian, put it away and go for your walk.'

'The new groom has come, so I ride to-day,' said Vivian, wearily. 'He's Morton's brother.'

The new groom was in reality the actor, Alfred de Lancy, whose guineas had been all-powerful with the lady's-maid. If poor, ignorant women look about for promising male fish to be landed by making the most of their opportunities, faces, and figures, why should not poor talented men, who are just as much adventurers in their way, do the same?

Vivian Branscombe, the beauty and heiress combined, pleased his taste, indeed he was madly in love with her. She had never given another thought to the hare-brained letter he had sent her.

It had occurred to De Lancy that if he could only be brought within shade of her magic presence, or feel the light, springy foot on his palm as he flung her into the saddle, he might have an opportunity of worshipping and secretly watching over a woman he could never possibly have met in the society in which she moved.

'Take my advice, Vivian, and walk; it will do you more good,' said her step-mother kindly. 'Just a nice stroll through the park, and you'll feel quite another being.'

Vivian had grown of late remarkably

obedient.   Her narrow eyes opened a little wider as she returned to her room in sheer self-amazement.

'What has come to me?' muttered the girl.   'I've actually given over quarrelling with Mrs Branscombe.'

She forgot to wonder if she resembled in every point and detail the figure of the last new fashion-plate—forgot how the wind or dust might affect her complexion, and summoning her maid, selected a simple black velvet costume trimmed with sable, and hat to match, and thus attired, sallied forth towards the park, at a time when, as the papers say, 'everybody who is anybody is out of town.'

Just as she was crossing the road leading to Hyde Park, her crimson silk lace-trimmed parasol up, although there was a very sickly-looking sun in the heavens—a bilious, sour-faced sun, shining as if he begrudged his light and warmth, especially in enlivening poor old London—she saw an ill-tempered, dark and swarthy face coming too close to hers to be pleasant.

With her Maltese pet, Skye, at her heels, her three-guinea parasol, her ten-button gloves, and seven-guinea hat—Vivian knew she was superb.

But she was easily frightened now.   Her

heart beat quickly, till she saw the nose of
a very small terrier peeping behind the man's
arm. This youthful canine specimen reassured her. The man only wanted, of
course, to sell the dog.

'Might yer ladyship wish to buy a little
dawg?' asked the man, holding the terrier
in turn by the ear, tail, and leg.

'I don't want any dogs,' said Vivian
haughtily, lifting her chin.

Lord Portmore had given her Skye the
last season. He was a duchess's pet, whom
the large man had purchased at an alarming
sacrifice of blue china.

As she spoke, she caught up her favourite
and crossed rapidly over the road—ladies
generally do rush on to the opposite pathway
when irritated and incensed.

But, to her horror, the man, nothing
abashed, followed.

'If you annoy me further I shall speak to
a policeman,' said Vivian, turning hot and
cold.

'Beg pardon, yer ladyship,' said her enemy,
'but I seed ye a walkin' with a little stiff
old party in a large bonnet the other day,
and so I made free to ask ye, if ye won't
buy the dawg, to take a bit of a note to
'er. I'm 'er son, yer ladyship, come back
from the war.'

'Certainly not,' said Vivian, angrily shaking herself, but with a certain nervous trembling of the lips. 'She never had any son.'

'Oh, then yer ladyship knows 'er, I can see, and ye won't buy the little dawg? There, take 'im for ten guineas, miss. He's cheap, an' a beauty, an' a horniment to any droring-room or carriage in the kingdom.'

Vivian hesitated; her heart again beating rapidly. The mystery, the hateful secret Mrs Sidewing had half-threatened her with, was it here revived? She would rather pay then and there for this hideous little terrier —a mongrel, she was sure, with painted legs and tail—than touch that dirty folded piece of paper, or convey it to Mrs Sidewing from this miserable-looking tramp; then curiosity got the better of her resolve.

'What does he want; what can he have to say to nurse?' thought Vivian, flushing crimson. 'And how will it affect *me?*'

'If you are really her son,' said Vivian, warily mastering her agitation, 'I don't mind buying the little dog out of charity.'

She opened her Russian leather purse, counted out ten sovereigns, handed them to the man, receiving in exchange the black, shiny-coated terrier and that sinister, ill-folded note.

Vivian went home in a strangely excited

state—a fever of desperation had seized her —she could have sobbed like a child. Why had she bought this hideous little terrier that had twice fought her darling Skye, and been jeered at and stoned by all the little vulgar boys she met, and why be holding that ominous piece of paper sealed with the odious red wax?

Sitting in her white and gold boudoir, her ringed hands pressed to her temples, Vivian knew danger threatened her, that a shadow dogged her steps, a spectre called Fear turning all her joys and hopes into dust and ashes.

She could not rise above an influence, at once searching and indefinable, that harassed her shallow brain, and made even conceit lose its self-satisfaction.

Something sooner or later would be revealed, and all waiting is torment to women of her temperament. She broke the seal with a reckless despair of consequences that must have been tragic in a grander soul, and this is what she read :—

'MARM,—I done it at last. Meet me at korner of V. Batt's Chapell Toosday night, an I'll prove my words.'

'Done what?' echoed Vivian, closing the note with trembling fingers. 'O heaven! what is this mystery hidden from me, of which this man and this woman alone hold the clue ? '

She lighted a taper, melted the wax, sealed it down again, and rang the bell. Would the day ever come when there would be no bells to ring, no servants to scold, no grand pianos to deal savage blows through chords that crashed under the fierce touch, no fifty-guinea costumes, no men to torture, or women to madden ? Extremes meet, reflected poor Vivian, whose portraits were selling well, and who had been positively driven to flirt with her singing master as a distraction. Vivian had not perfectly mastered the shake, though she paid a guinea a lesson, and Signor Adagio told her she might arrive at great things. Vivian had been quite amiable and condescending to every one since her empire had been threatened, and the supple Italian, whose mother was a washerwoman in Naples, could charge her six shillings for each of his own compositions, selling elsewhere at sixpence, without her being aware of the overcharge, he flattering himself, meanwhile, that the beautiful Miss Branscombe had found his fiery gaze, fine wristbands, octave passages, and passionate crescendos too much for her imagination.

'Tell Mrs Sidewing I want to see her,' said Vivian to the servant who answered her summons. ' Yes, and bring me some strong tea. I'll not take any luncheon to-day ; and tell every one who calls that I'm out.'

It was nothing unusual for Vivian, when in her tantrums or hysterics, to retire to her bed for three days, and giving herself the air of an invalid, take chicken-broth or beef-tea freely, till she felt so bored by working point-lace in sweet seclusion that she often dressed herself hastily, ordered her horse, and rode for three hours, taking a warm bath on her return, that seemed quite to restore her good humour.

But the days of caprice were over ; a new doubt had come that fastened on rose diamonds, and spoke in hard-breathed accents, and was terrible aud prophetic, re-quiring, maybe soon all her stratagems, worldliness, and tact to defeat.

Mrs Sidewing came in herself with the tea on a costly silver salver,—the tea service was of the finest Dresden,—a present from Mr Branscombe to Vivian on her last birthday. She began to prize for the first time all these tokens of affection and of wealth.

' Ah, is it you, nurse ?' said Vivian, lean-ing back languidly in her chair, feeling like some condemned criminal obliged to look grateful and penitent when she is longing to be obstreperous.

It was wonderful how Vivian's manner had changed, and with what respect she treated the woman she had once so bitterly reviled.

' Yes, dearie, it's me.   So your 'ead aches, does it ?   Maybe the walk was too much for you to-day ? '

Vivian eyed her keenly, a new terror moving her to the depths of her soul.

' Nurse,' she said, in a whisper, spreading her hands before her face, ' I fear you.   I don't know why, but ever since the diamond necklace went, and you spoke to me in that fierce, strange way, I've had no rest or peace of mind.   It's hardly fair, is it ? ' said Vivian, faintly, her thin lips twitching through the effort to keep back her tears, ' that I should be punished like this for something I've never done or deserved ?   I'm so tired of never sleeping, but lying awake hour after hour, watching the light steal through the blinds, thinking of the necklace, and what you said, and what I heard Bob whisper before I fainted.'

Again that ghastly gleam of malice came into the nurse's eyes,—a dreadful dazed look that made Vivian cry out as if something were strangling her,—as if the nurse were trampling out a feeble life that had yet been dangerous to her own existence.

She pillowed Vivian's aching head on her

breast, smoothing back her hair, and fondling her, and Vivian submitted because she no longer dared resist.

'Never *you mind nothink about him,*' said the nurse in a whisper. 'He'll never worry us any more, dearie. He's gone back to Ameriky, the villain, and 'ull never set foot again on English shores.'

'Was he cruel to you, nurse?' asked Vivian, holding back the note.

No, she was too frightened to give it to her just yet. She must wait and question further.

'Cruel ain't the word, miss. It was nag, nag all day. Nagging at me for knowing nothink, and not being fit to receive 'is friends, —and a precious set they were, too,—and nagging 'cos I was ugly and pock-marked,— which, miss, is an affliction sent from above as we can't avoid,—and nagging 'cos he could get no money out o' me to spend on his hactresses,—a set o' painted daws, I'd teach them,' said Mrs Sidewing, bringing her strong hand fiercely down on the dainty white and gold table where Vivian, with pale lips, sat.

'You must have got very tired of such ill-treatment, nurse?' said Vivian, cautiously, after a pause.

A new passion seized the woman, the more

alarming as it contrasted with her usually quiet, repressed manner.

'I loved 'im once,—oh, how I loved him! He was a fine, tall, 'andsome man, but when he married me for the sake of a bit o' money master gave me for doin' my duty to you and 'is first lady wot left 'im, then Bob changed. Poverty and neglect are bad to bear when you're young, dearie, aren't they? an' to 'ave to go back to service through a gay 'usband, why, it 'ud rile anybody. I've sat an' waited an' seen 'im with them girls an' their painted cheeks outside the theayter, an' I could a killed ere a one of 'em. I knew it was my money Bob spent like water. I spoke to a magistrate. "It's very 'ard," I says, "sir, to 'ave a man take yer money and spend it on other women," I says, "an' me not be able to get rid of 'im neither," for I couldn't prove nothink, and he never struck me.'

Still the note shook in Vivian's delicate hand. What was the deed here foreshadowed? Could it be murder? And could this objectionable husband be the victim?

'When I went out to-day,' said Vivian, pausing between her words, and sipping her tea, 'a rough fellow spoke to me, and he— he said he knew you—that he was your son. Of course I knew that was false, because you only had a little daughter'—Vivian's voice lingered here and vibrated—'who died; but still I bought the little dog of him, and he gave me this.'

She held the note up, the pink shell-like tints of her complexion paling to ashy whiteness, and threw it on the table.

Mrs Sidewing examined the seal, saw, as she believed, that the red wax had not been tampered with, and put the note in her pocket.

'Read it,' said Vivian, hoarsely, yielding to a sudden impulse under the excitement of pain,—physical pain that dragged at her heart, and almost stopped its beating.

'No, miss, it 'ull keep,' said Mrs Sidewing, coolly. 'I never worrits over nothink, I don't.'

'But I have read it,' said Vivian, haughtily, a deadly sickness overpowering her. 'I know what it contains. It alludes to *some deed* that has been done at last.'

'What!' cried Mrs Sidewing, staggering backwards.

'Ah, you tremble now! The deed, nurse, the awful deed! The necklace went; I bore that and said nothing, but now—O heaven!' smiting her hands,—'I must know. Is it,' standing up and lowering her voice, 'is it murder?'

Still Mrs Sidewing never spoke, but she, too had paled to a deathly hue; her lips worked, but she was silent.

'Speak!' said Vivian, imperiously, clutching her shoulder, her old hatred mastering her, and giving her unnatural strength and courage; 'don't you know you're a servant, paid by my father, and must obey? Speak! I'll make you, or expose you. I'll send for papa and Mrs Branscombe and the servants. You know me; I'm no saint; a thief you are; but a murderess—no, no, no, it's too horrible. But speak; for if I am myself to be ruined and destroyed by you in the world which I love, I swear before heaven that I'll have the truth out of you this day!'

The nurse seized the paper, tried to read the first few lines, but failed, and with a wailing cry fell like a stone at Vivian's feet.

# CHAPTER XV.

## A CRUEL VENGEANCE.

'AND so Timon is at last enslaved,' M. Lepelletier is saying, leaning back in one of the easiest arm-chairs he can find in the library at Staplefield Hall. 'And Venus, after all, is to be worshipped. Ah! ah! *parole d'honneur*, it was a pretty scene! Where had vanished your gloom then, *mon cher*? Once I be-lieved in your cynicism, now I cannot doubt your hypocrisy.'

Leonard never takes his eyes off the changes in this dark face, gleaming fitfully in the afternoon shadows; but he does not speak. Those soft crimson lips, that golden-bronze hair, the sweet subjection, the wilful-ness and romance of Nellie's love, are fascina-tions he has begun at last to brood over.

'Pretty, isn't she?' the cold voice goes on, 'but most decidedly wild; and where could you find roses to compare with her lips and blushes? Are you not grateful to me for bringing Nellie Raymond to Brooksmere? Suppose I've got a benevolent fit on me— call it caprice—what you will—and that I'm interested in the girl and have taken a fancy to her.'

Still no answer.

M. Lepelletier did not admire this silence; his pale face grew a trifle paler, he lit a cigar and smoked on silently.

Presently he rose, and came over to where Captain Mallandaine was seated.

'And now, Leonard, a word with you on another topic,' he said quietly; 'the motive that brought me once more under your roof.'

Something like a vicious scowl stole over his long brows, that deepened the furrow between his eyes. Leonard laid down his cigar, looking his enemy straight in the face.

'Ah, *mon cher*,' cried Lepelletier, 'this will never do. I want to make you talk, and you persistently decline to answer.'

'I've been doing my best to cut you for years,' answered the Captain, coolly lifting his eyes and meeting the other's insolent stare.

'Another insult,' cried the Frenchman, starting to his feet. '*Diable!* this is insufferable.'

'Why don't you challenge me to a duel, Lepelletier? You're fond of frightening editors and raw boys. I will tell you—because you dare not.'

'Dare not!' he echoed, looking dangerous, but keeping quiet. 'This is mere childish fooling, beneath my contempt. I can strike you in a far more vulnerable part still. I can prove who you are hiding away in the west wing of Staplefield Hall, and one of the proudest families in Devonshire will have its skeleton dragged from its cupboard.'

'How would this affect or benefit you?'

'It is part of my revenge. I have learnt the truth. Your sister Aurelia is here concealed, and I have come to insist on an interview.'

'Insist?'

'Well, it comes to nearly the same thing. I intend to see Miss Mallandaine some time to-day, or I shall give notice to the authorities of the law that you are acting illegally.'

'And your motive?'

'Oh, *mon cher*, that is easily understood. When I loved your sister with an adoration approaching madness, and every thought was torment, both you and she insulted me in the most heartless manner possible. Now, when I still love and admire your sister, but hate her, too, I want to see what a wreck the scornful beauty has become.'

Leonard's face darkened still more.

'Trust me, Leonard, I shall be very gentle; I may not even speak. Confess she owes me some slight reparation for all the pangs of misery she has inflicted. Think of my jealousy and fury when Oscar de Beriot triumphed where I had failed, and won a heart that to me would have been the most prized treasure earth could have held.'

'Did you not have your revenge before? You could not bear your disappointment like a man, but like a demon. Who brought Signora Firmiani to De Beriot's lodgings, and made her sing to him, and study every art to bewitch and entrap him? You see, I am well informed.'

Lepelletier had puffed away coolly at his cigar, but here he again started to his feet on the point of denying the accusation.

'Yes,' said Leonard, in the cold voice that made feverish throbbings assail the other's brain, 'it was you—false friend—pitiless lover—unscrupulous foe. Madame Firmiani was at your mercy, and you left no stone unturned in aiding her to dazzle De Beriot. He swore this to me with his last breath— dying men speak the truth.'

'All's fair in love or war, *mon cher*,' said

the Frenchman, sipping his wine. ' I had
that one card to play, and I played it well.
I had but one weapon to strike with, and I
sent it home—to the heart.'

' Then why do you persist in haunting and
disturbing us ? My father was kind to you
when you were friendless, and received you
with hospitality and consideration ; you fell
passionately in love with my sister Aurelia ;
you say you date all your sufferings from the
hour in which you were rejected. It was not
your poverty we loathed, but your principles
—your poverty has gone, your principles
remain.'

There was a gleam of fury in Leonard's
expression, a scintillating fire such as may be
seen springing from iron beaten by a hammer.

' *Diantre!* But you are candid.'

'When my sister was engaged to your
cousin, and the marriage settled on, you
brought temptation, craft, and all your in-
fernal juggleries to suborn a weak-minded
man, and you succeeded ; you looked on
coolly, like a gambler watches a game in
which human souls, not gold, are lost and
won ; you studied every move of a base
revenge, and you knew what sort of nature
Aurelia had—the deep wells of emotion, the
bright, poetical fancies, the sensitive tenderness.
Yes, you had read all these like open pages.'

Lepelletier folded his arms, and looked dreamily across the swaying boughs of the avenue of chestnuts beyond the lawn.   That cold voice had a menace, and he had no idea that Captain Mallandaine had so perfectly comprehended his actions.

'And now the sequel —Aurelia's mind slowly gives way—I do not say she is insane (it is false), but heart-broken.   De Beriot has acted treacherously.   I insist on reparation, and I will do him justice so far, that he was no coward, for when I smote him across the face, he was quite ready to fight me—a duel was the consequence, in which he was mortally wounded, and admitted the justice of his doom.   You are the cause of all this misery and bloodshed, and now have the audacity to say you have triumphed, and insist on seeing the poor dying girl.'

Lepelletier laughs cynically.

'I suppose you call that strong English?' he said, coming close to Leonard with noiseless step.   'Yes, I have endeavoured to crush and degrade you all ; her anguish is my triumph.   I swore she should suffer agony of agonies.   *Ciel!*  Was I to let her go free, and die myself inch by inch ?   Always hatred, always irony, always contempt directed against me.   It was a war.'

'Lepelletier, you are a most unmitigated villain.'

'Still strong language. I said to myself, this lovely girl, with her poet's soul and peerless beauty, shall daily feel like I—the hurricane of fevered thought—I, though she hates me, shall yet be her fate—I, though less than the dust under her feet, still claim her sacrifice. I exult in her despair. Yes, Leonard, I have waited day by day, month by month, sustained by this one thought. She despised me. It was not that she could not love me, but she made no allowance for my jealousy and passion, which she regarded as insults, that I could never forgive, and through that have I made her degradation and yours complete.'

'I had hoped,' said Leonard still coldly, but the fire kindling again in his eyes, 'that Aurelia might have died ere she beheld your face again.'

'You laid your plans well; you schemed to mislead me, but you find I have learnt the truth, and I shall see her—this very hour.'

'You are wealthy,' said Leonard, making one last appeal, 'why not let the good fortune lately showered on you suffice, and leave those whose lives you have ruined in peace?'

'*Desolé* not to be able to take your view of

the matter, but I have set my mind on seeing your sister. You are right, I am wealthy, but what of that? Wealth came to me by the merest chance. An obstinate old fool, who had neglected me all through my best days, quarrels with those natural toadies around him—his relatives, and endows me with his money. I never could have made a fortune, and have none of the elements which constitute the successful men, the Crœsi of this world.'

Leonard crossed the room and bent over his enemy.

' Be generous for once, resist this desire to see my sister, trouble us no more, but leave her to die in peace.'

A crimson flush mounted to the other's cheek.

' No, Leonard, no. Am I to be baulked of my revenge? I must see her this very day.'

' Very well,' answered Leonard, 'you shall see her, but—'

' Take me to her,' cried Lepelletier hoarsely, 'and at once. Oh, my love, my angel, will you be changed, I wonder? The smile gone from your lips, the radiance from your gaze?'

His words tortured Leonard beyond endurance.

'Wait,' he said, as Lepelletier made for the door.

' I must have my triumph; I have earned it.'

. ' Villain !' muttered Leonard, between his teeth, ' I warn you, if you persevere in these visits and your cruel conduct, I will find means to unearth your past, to unveil your crimes. People shall shrink from and avoid you. Remember, you have been black-balled at two West-end clubs ; your continental rovings also terminated suddenly. When I was at Munich last year, a woman was found mysteriously murdered on her doorstep in the early dawn ; it was known you had been her lover. Will you recollect how you left Munich ?'

'*Pardieu!* we are wasting time,' said Lepelletier, shrugging his shoulders, his complexion assuming a leaden hue. ' These are mere idle ravings—you are talking nonsense. Come and take me to the room in which Aurelia weeps.'

Without another word, Captain Mallandaine led the way through a long dark corridor, at the end of which was a heavy baize-covered door.

Lepelletier paled still more as they approached the entrance to this west wing. They crossed the picture galleries and turned to the right. Here they came upon a wall in the middle of which was a door.   Leonard pushed this door open, and entered slowly.

'And now behold your work,' he whispered, pointing to a white-robed figure in a distant corner of the room.

She was sitting before a piano as they entered, her hands hanging lifelessly over the keys.   Never was ruin more complete.   She rose to welcome Leonard as usual, but seeing Lepelletier by his side, she uttered a loud and piercing scream, clinging to her brother's arm in pallid agitation.

Aurelia's aspect bore that unmistakable air of lassitude and exhaustion in which is the awful weakness of decay—weakness produced by long, sleepless nights of fever and despair.

There is something in her grief-worn look and spectral aspect that has strange charm for Lepelletier's imagination ; his eyes grow glassy while regarding hers.

But for him she would have been Oscar de Beriot's wife ; but for him that breast pierced with the fatal sword-thrust, and lying cold in death, must have pillowed her dark head. This helpless anguish is too terrible to witness long.

'Do you know me ?' he asks, approaching her.

'Yes,' Aurelia answers, looking into the pale wicked face of her destroyer, 'and I am dying very fast—I am going away; you will not smile at me much longer.' Then to Leonard, 'Why did you bring this man here to me?'

'Aurelia,' said Lepelletier, still with that horrible smiling hatred in his eyes, in which was ill-disguised pain, ' I told you when you despised my love that you would one day regret it. Do you remember? We were in the garden alone, and the sun was setting. I implored your pity, your compassion; I told you my love was self-destroying, and that, rejected, it might also scheme your ruin. Mine was the passion that leads a man to murder the woman he adores, and kiss her when dead, and put her arms about his neck, and die too.' He paused, breathing hard. 'You disregarded the danger about your path, you saw no tragedy beneath —you were the spoilt, proud beauty; why should you care for a poor man, ugly, too, and despised? But you were walking all the time on the edge of a grave.'

'Leonard, spare me this,' cried Aurelia, throwing herself into her brother's arms.

Lepelletier's voice had now sunk to a low, dull murmur.

'Why should you value my love? You did not, and you are destroyed. You thought me submissive under your contempt and dis-

pleasure; no, no—never. I vowed then that
if you were not mine—my wife to cherish
and adore, that you should be none other's.
Have I not kept my word?'

She looked at him in horrified surprise;
her lips moved, but she made no reply; she
was too weak to suffer more.

'So have I plotted against you, and held
you in my power all along. I killed your
mind—I could picture your tears and anguish,
your lonely nights and days. You would
have been a brilliant woman—a poet, a
writer. English, too. Well, I hated all that
—I claimed you as a sacrifice. Is this not
revenge?

Aurelia had wrenched herself from her
brother's grasp—supernatural strength seemed
granted her at this crisis—she rose, her steps
no longer languid, and crossed over to where
Lepelletier stood, his arms folded in a gloomy
attitude by the window, and she laid her
hand on his arm.

Her light touch thrilled him, tremors
passed through his frame.

'And are you content?' she asked in her
silvery, tearful tones. 'Does it make you
any happier? Do you recollect how we
nursed you after that fall from your horse,
and I sat and read with you, and brought
you fresh flowers every day? You, I see,

have brought me a red rose.' She lifted her hand and drew a flower from his coat. It was a half-crushed rosebud, which he had forgotten had been fastened there by Nellie.

'You were my idol,' he burst out passionately. 'O heavens, that I should love a woman so!'

'If there's any pity or remorse in your heart, think of it—think of it. And now, Leonard, take me away; I'm tired, and must rest.'

As Leonard drew her towards him, her eyes grew more dim, and with a faint cry, she stretched out her arms and fainted.

'Are you not satisfied?' asked Leonard, coldly, pointing to the door. 'Go—all malice must have its limits, even yours.'

Lepelletier staggered to the door, stood irresolute for a second, then closed it softly, and was on the point of yielding to a great burst of emotion in the form of tears when he saw Nellie coming across the lawn towards him.

'After all, if Aurelia had loved me, she would have been always tremendously tragic, and that is such a deuce of a bore,' said the light-hearted Frenchman characteristically, checking his tears. 'Laura, I am sure, will be the same, but then Laura loves me, and is ready for any madness—these English women

are so absurdly intense. Talk about Medea!
What a time that poor beggar Jason must
have had of it, to be sure!'

M. Lepelletier was so grateful to Nellie
for thus coming to the rescue at a painful
crisis, that he went forward hastily to greet
her.

'Well, child, what is it?' he asked.

'A lady has called to see you,' she
answered, while as she spoke Leonard came
down the steps reading a letter.

Captain Mallandaine found it a very
strange and mysterious communication indeed. He had to read it over several times
before he understood its contents, and then
thought Branscombe must be growing more
eccentric than ever.

This letter alluded to Leonard's bravery
in having saved his (the writer's) life on the
Alps some years ago, in terms of almost
fervent gratitude. He also entreated
Leonard to return at once to London, and
wound up by saying his health was by no
means satisfactory, and that he intended to
travel.

'A lady!' echoed Lepelletier, not altogether unprepared for this news. 'What a
reception is in store for me!'

He walked quickly towards the cottage,
and saw a well-cut profile, which he recog-

nised as that of Laura Branscombe. She was thickly veiled, and was standing by the mantelpiece in Faculty's best parlour.

'Gustave,' Laura cried, throwing off her veil, 'I could bear it no longer. I was told you were seen with a young, golden-haired girl, whom you had met at a circus.'

'And your husband, *chere* madame?' he inquired, enjoying her agitation.

'He has gone away for a few days. Vivian is at home. Ah! *they* must never know—'

'Of course not,' answered Lepelletier, laconically. 'How could you be so wild, so imprudent, Laura, as to come at all?'

'Ah, why?' she said. 'And *you* can ask me that?'

Still tragedy, still agony! When would it end? Whenever, of course, he pleased.

'Ah, *ma chere*, you take it too much to heart,' he said tenderly. 'You'll be quite ill with all this agitation.'

'Ill, Gustave! I shall positively die if this sort of thing goes on much longer. I thought love was cruel enough to bear, but what is it to the pangs of jealousy?'

His shallow nature was just stirred on the surface as he listened to the depth of her sad utterance.

'And then my remorse!' clasping her hands. 'The dreadful struggle, day by day, to bear up, and be patient, forget you, and endure my husband.'

'Oh, he's a horrid little cad, *ma chere*,' said the lover. 'Don't talk of him.'

'But I am not heartless, Gustave. I have submitted to the conventionalities of society, and passed years of cold alienation from Mr Branscombe, believing in honour and duty till I met you. One glance, one smile, and the very essence of my soul fled to you, and has been yours to torture. What devil gave you this hold over me? You are not a good man. I am sure you are cruel and callous, and yet I am fascinated, enthralled, and lost—'

'*Pardi*, I've been devoted,' he said, with the faintest shrug. 'Now, *ma belle*—for beautiful you are, and mine also, or soon will be—go home quietly without a scene, and as befits a woman of education and the world, to Prince's Gate. Your husband may be on the watch. No golden-haired rival need you fear. Besides, I detest girls. To my mind, a woman isn't worth a fig under forty.'

'Gustave, have you any pity? Are you still cold or angry with me?'

'Oh, *mon ange*, you're charming in your new character of a jealous woman; the gloomy passions suit your style.'

'It must be the climate makes the English

take life so seriously,' he reflected, hoping Mrs Branscombe would catch the express.

'And when shall we—shall I see you again ?'

'To-morrow without a doubt.'

He bent down and kissed her on the mouth.

'A mouth made for songs and love,' he whispered.

'If you forsake me or are false I shall die,' Laura said, with a sweet wintry smile, drawing her veil over her face, and fastening her sables and velvet. 'I've something proud in me, Gustave. I could not sink to the level of those I despise.'

'You've a long and tedious journey, Laura,' glancing at his watch.

'But I've seen you, and now farewell,' she cried, holding out her hand. 'When love becomes ungovernable, it must be very near to death,' she murmured. 'Don't you think so ? And that may be expiation. Yesterday I read these lines :—

> " Sweet is true love, though given in vain—in vain ;
> And sweet is death that puts an end to pain."

If, Gustave, an innocent child thought this, what must a guilty woman feel ? I shall be ready to meet my doom.'

She had glided past him, waving her hands, and was soon lost from view.

'*Ciel!* It would never do to trifle with her,' he muttered, then laughing and touching his brow. '*Parole d'honneur!* Another lunatic!'

END OF VOL. I.

COLSTON AND SON, PRINTERS, EDINBURGH.